SUGAR CREEK GANG
THE
PALM TREE MANHUNT

SUGAR CREEK GANG
THE
PALM TREE MANHUNT

Original title:
Sugar Creek Gang on Palm Tree Island

Paul Hutchens

MOODY PRESS • CHICAGO

ISBN 0-8024-4808-9

Eighth Printing, 1982

1

IT WAS THE SNOWIEST DAY I had ever seen when Poetry came over to my house with his sled, pulling it along after him, with snowflakes as big as pullets' eggs falling all around him. He was wading along in his boots down our road. As soon as I saw him, I knew right away that he had something important to tell me. I stepped out onto our back porch with my bare head, and Mom called and told me to come in and get my cap on or I'd catch my death of cold.

Poetry waved his arm and yelled, "Hey! Bill!"

"What?" I yelled back out across the snow to him.

"Wait just a minute!" He came puffing up to our front gate, lifted the latch, shoved the gate open, pushing it kind of hard against the snow which had drifted there, came on through, pulling his sled after him. Then he turned around, pushing the gate shut.

While he was wading up to our back porch, I was in the house getting my cap on with its fur-lined ear muffs, pulling on my boots and all the different clothes which Mom said I had to wear or I'd catch my death of cold. Then I opened the door and came out into the snowflakes which were still as big as pullets' eggs and were coming down like goose feathers. It was as if a great big dirigible full of goose feathers had burst up there in the sky somewhere.

The first thing I did was to scoop up a handful of nice fresh, clean, soft snow and make it into a ball the size of a baseball and throw it whizzety-sizzle out across the barnyard at our old black and white cat who was sitting and mewing like everything on the side of the barn where there wasn't so much snow, acting like she was disgusted with the weather, even though it wasn't very cold.

I didn't have the least idea what the snowball was going to do. In fact, I'd have been shocked if I had known it was going to fly so high and also that the very minute it got to the corner of the barn a brand-new boy who had moved into our neighborhood was going to come dashing around just in time to get socked right kersquash on the top of his brand-new bright red cap.

Certainly I didn't know that brand-new boy had a temper as fiery as mine; that he was a fierce fighter and was bigger than I was and older and was a bully, 'cause I'd never seen him.

But—well, the very minute I saw what was going to happen, I felt a funny tingling sensation go zippering up my spine to the roots of my red hair and I knew there was going to be trouble.

Dad had told me there was a new family moving into the house down beyond the mouth of the branch, and that there was a boy who might want to join the Sugar Creek Gang. I hadn't liked the idea very well, 'cause any new boy in our neighborhood nearly always meant that somebody in our gang wouldn't like him, and there was bound to be some kind of an interesting fight before we found out whether he was going to run the gang—or was just going to try to.

But there he was—and he was running head on into my innocent snowball!

Well, when you don't do a thing on purpose, you don't feel very guilty for having done it.

I don't think I ever saw a snowball fly faster in my life than that one did—and I don't think I ever missed my mark so far in my life—or did I? Anyway, the thing happened. The next thing I knew, that hard snowball, which I'd made as hard almost as a baseball, crashed kersquash-wham-thud right on the top of that new boy's head and the snowball and the red cap landed in a snowdrift which the wind had piled high at the corner of the barn.

That's how the Sugar Creek Gang came to find out right away whether the new guy was going to be friendly or not—and he wasn't.

There he was, standing, looking astonished and funny and mad and surprised and everything else. He let out a yell and six or seven swear words which made me mad right away 'cause Dad had taught me not to swear and I had had several lickings for doing it when I was little and didn't know any better—and then I had quit for good. So that new guy's swearing made me so mad I was all ready to fight even before I knew I was going to have to.

I say I had to. I mean I really did, or else get the stuffin's knocked out of me.

He swung around quick, made a dive for his cap in the snowdrift, got it, shook it out like a dog shaking a rat, while our old black and white cat made a dive for the barn door at the same time. Then that guy made a snowball quicker than you can say "Jack Robinson Crusoe and his Man Friday," swung back his right arm and threw the snowball straight at my head. Before I could duck, I'd been hit kersquash-wham-thud myself and was seeing stars, and also feeling the cold air on my head as my cap flew off. Then I made a dive for my cap, shook it out and had it back on in less than a half jiffy.

Well, that cold snowball was too hot for me, and I was half mad in half a jiffy, so I yelled back, "You big lummox! I didn't aim to hit you. I was throwing that snowball at our old cat!"

But you know, he didn't get it straight! He yelled back at me, "I'm not a big lummox, and I'm not an old cat!"

And without intending to—being a little mixed up in my mind because of being half angry, I yelled back at him, "You are too!" And the fight was on, first with words and then with fists. And while we were still mad at each other, I couldn't even feel myself getting hurt. It's only afterward, after you've quit enjoying the fight, that you feel hurt.

That big lummox started on the run toward me, scooping up snowballs and throwing them at me on the way. And I was doing the same thing to him. He was calling me a redhead and I was calling him a big lummox. And pretty soon he threw a snowball at me which hit me before it left his hand, which means he hit me with his fist! And then I was seeing red stars, and fighting like everything and rolling in the snow and he was doing the same thing. I didn't even remember Poetry was there until I heard him saying, "Atta boy, Bill! Let him have it!"

9

Then I woke up to the fact that I was having a fight and that Dad had told me I was not to have any more fights—anyway, not to start any and that I could fight only if the other guy started it.

Even while I was washing that new guy's ears with snow and smearing his face with more snow, I couldn't remember which one of us had started the fight. Then I heard Dad call from the house or somewhere, and that's how I happened to get licked. The next thing I knew I was plunging head first into a drift. Then I was down under that guy and couldn't breathe and was trying to yell and was choking and smothering and everything and I couldn't turn over or anything. For a jiffy I didn't know anything except that it seemed like a million years before I could get my breath again. I'd been hit right in the stomach just before I went down, and there just wasn't any wind left in me, and I couldn't breathe anyway. So I gave up without even knowing I was doing it, and the fight was over for a while.

Just then Mom came out and stood on our back porch and called, "Boys, I've just finished baking a blackberry pie. Would you like some?"

Well, Poetry heard that before any of the rest of us did, and yelled back, "Sure!"

10

2

IT WAS REALLY TOO BAD that our perfectly innocent fight had to break up right at that minute. I knew very well that if I could have started over again, I could have licked the stuffin's out of that great big guy. But when a fight ends in an invitation to eat blackberry pie, a fellow doesn't feel so bad about it.

I unrolled myself from that snowdrift and up onto my knees and then up onto my feet, Poetry helping me a little. I couldn't see too well because of some crazy old tears that got in my eyes along with the snow.

After I was up, I got my hat and shook the snow off it and out of it at the same time. Then I just stood there and panted and glared at that big fat lummox who was as tall as Big Jim, the leader of our gang, and was almost as fat as Poetry. I was still mad although he had knocked the wind and some of the temper out of me at the same time.

Poetry grunted as he stooped over and picked up

11

his sled rope. The new guy and I stood there, looking at our caps and panting and knocking snow off
ourselves. Every now and then we looked at each
other at the same time and kind of walked around
a little, and looked at each other mad-like. I was
thinking all the time about where I should have hit
him and hadn't and where I'd do it next time. I
still couldn't see straight, so I yelled at him, with
tears in my voice, "You—you great big lummox.
You hit me in the stomach—"

That started Poetry, who is always quoting a
poem of some kind or other, to quoting one right
that minute. So he said—quoting from the "Night
Before Christmas":

> A little round man with a little round belly
> That shook when he laughed like a bowlful
> of jelly.

But it wasn't funny.
"Keep still!" I said to Poetry.
Then the new guy spoke up and said saucily to
Poetry, "So *you're* the one they told me was a poet.
Well, you remind me of a poem too—

> You're a poet, and you don't know it,
> And if you had whiskers you'd be a go-at!

Just then a snowball came sizzling from behind
our barn and crashed against the new guy's cap,

and it fell off again and in a snowdrift. And it was Circus himself who had thrown the snowball. By the time I could turn around and look to see which one of the gang it was, he had changed from walking on his feet, and was on his hands, walking right toward us.

The gang had planned to go to the cave that afternoon and then go through the cave up to Old Man Paddler's cabin in the hills. The other end of the cave was in the basement of his old clapboard-roofed house, which looked like the house Abraham Lincoln was born in.

In another jiffy we heard a yell from near our front gate, and it was a little guy dressed in a mackinaw and a fur hat. He was carrying a stick, and I knew it was Little Jim himself.

"Hi, Little Jim!" I yelled to him and decided not to even look at the big lummox again.

"Hi," Little Jim called back. Then he yelled to the new guy and said, "Hi, Shorty! Mom says you can ride with us tomorrow if you want to."

In just another jiffy, Little Jim came tumbling up to where we were, stopping every now and then to make tracks in the snow which looked like rabbit tracks with his stick. In just a jiffy another snowball came sizzling from a different direction, and this time it was little spindle-legged Dragonfly whose nose turns south at the end and whose eyes are bigger than his head, almost. He came shuffling his way through the snow from around the other side of the house.

In less than a jiffy or two, all the Sugar Creek Gang was there—Big Jim with his fuzzy moustache; Little Jim with his stick, who was the best Christian in the gang and maybe in the whole world; Dragonfly with his dragonflylike eyes; barrel-shaped Poetry who knew one hundred poems by heart; Circus with his monkey face, who was our acrobat; and last of all, Little Tom Till, whose hair was as red as mine, whose temper was as hot as mine, and whose freckles were just a little thicker on his face than mine. That was all of us.

Well, the thing was, what to do with the new boy.

"What's your name?" I said to the big lummox, forgetting I didn't want to talk to him at all. He was making a snowball and getting over his temper at the same time. And at the same time I was getting partway over mine.

He didn't answer until after he'd thrown the snowball at Mixy, our cat who was out in the shadow of the barn again. Then he answered just as the snowball left his hands, and the words sounded like they were being thrown hard straight at me.

"Shorty Long!" he said.

"What! Shorty Long!" I exclaimed.

14

"Sure!" Little Jim piped up. "His name is Shorty Long, and he is going to ride along with all of the Foote family tomorrow to Sunday school and church." That goes to show that Little Jim was about the only one of the Sugar Creek Gang who had the right attitude toward the new boy who had moved into our neighborhood.

Well, it wasn't any more than half a jiffy when all of us boys heard Mom call again, "Hurry up, you boys, if you want a piece of blackberry pie!"

Well, I turned around and looked up to the house at Mom and I saw the most astonished expression on her face. You see, when she had first called us there were only three of us, and that would have meant only three pieces of pie for her to spare; but when she called this time there were eight of us, including Shorty Long, who looked like he could have eaten three pieces himself and still have room for several more. Two whole pies would be spoiled—and I wouldn't have any for dinner tomorrow, I thought.

It didn't take all of us boys very long to get up to where that pie was waiting for us, and it certainly didn't take any of us very long to get our pieces of pie eaten. Mom brought them out and let us eat them right there in the snow rather than take us all in the house and get snow all over her floor, which she nearly always mopped especially clean on Saturdays so it would be that way on Sundays.

Pretty soon the gang, including the new boy, was on its way through the woods, wading through the snow, following the footpath which goes to the spring. There wasn't any path visible, but we knew exactly where it was supposed to be, so we made a new one. Next thing we knew we were up along the edge of Sugar Creek not far from the old sycamore tree. All of a sudden Poetry, who was walking beside me—both of us being ahead of the rest of the gang—said, "I've got a letter for Old Man Paddler. My dad got it at the post office. It's from Palm Tree Island."

"Palm Tree Island!" I said, and then I remembered that Old Man Paddler had a map of Palm Tree Island on the wall of his cabin, and that he was especially interested in that caterpillar-shaped island. None of the gang knew just why he was interested in it, but most of us had been secretly hoping that maybe the old man who had sent us all on a camping trip to the north woods one summer, and also had sent us all to Chicago and had paid for both trips himself, might some day decide to spend some of his money to send us down there to see what it is like to see a foreign missionary at work. The old man was especially interested in missionaries, and was always praying for them.

"Sure!" Poetry said as he pulled off one of his gloves with his teeth, reached into a pocket and pulled out a letter.

"Let me see it," I said and took it into my own hands.

"What's *Correo Aereo?*" I asked, looking at the strange stamp and the strange writing on the letter.

"Goose!" Poetry said. *"Correo Aereo* is Spanish for *Airmail,* of course. They wanted it to come in a hurry. It's an important letter."

Well, I let out a yell that brought all the gang running. "Look!" I cried. "An airmail letter from Palm Tree Island!"

While the gang was running through the snow to get to where I was, I noticed that the letter was postmarked *Palacia* which Poetry said was the capital of Palm Tree Island.

Pretty soon the gang had all come and had looked at the letter and had helped me make a lot of different kinds of noise. Then in a jiffy we were at the mouth of the cave where some of us who had brought our flashlights along, turned them on. The next thing we knew we were walking Indian fashion, which is one at a time, through that cave, stooping a little here and squeezing through a tight place there, on our way through the long cave up toward Old Man Paddler's cabin. It was a whole lot quicker to get to his cabin by going through the

17

cave than it would be by following the old snow-drift-covered wagon road around through the hills.

Well, pretty soon we came to a big wooden door which opened into the basement of Old Man Paddler's house.

Big Jim knocked a couple of times, then we heard a voice from upstairs say, "Who—who's there?" We knew it was Old Man Paddler's high-pitched, quavering voice. In my mind's eye I could see his long, white whiskers and his very gray eyes, only you couldn't always see his eyes because sometimes they were hidden behind the thick lenses of his glasses.

Pretty soon the basement door opened and all the gang was in the cellar and were climbing up the stairs and going through the trapdoor into his cabin. There was a swell fire crackling in the fireplace and hot water was sizzling on the stove; steam was coming out of the teakettle, making the windows all steamed up. And right there on the table was a panful of broken-up pieces of red sassafras roots which we were going to have made into sassafras tea in just a little while.

"A letter for you, Mr. Paddler," Poetry said politely, and took out of his pocket the airmail letter which had been postmarked *Palacia*, and handed it to the old man.

"Thank you, Poetry," he said. "Sit down, boys."

We did, only some of us didn't sit; we just flopped down on the floor in different directions, some of us sitting on chairs, some on the edges of chairs, and some just kind of propped up against the others. The old man put on his thick-lensed glasses which were almost as thick as magnifying glasses, and said, "Boys, if you will excuse me a minute—"

"Sure," some of us said.

3

THE GNARLED OLD FINGERS of the old man tore open the letter and I couldn't help but notice how much his hands trembled. I felt a queer lump in my throat, 'cause maybe the old man wasn't in as good health as he had been last year, and he might not live very much longer. Also right that minute while he was unfolding the letter and starting to read it, I remembered that he had told us once that he had put the Sugar Creek Gang into his will, which he had already made, and that some time when he died there would be something for each of us.

But none of the gang wanted him to die. Anyway, the kind old man was always giving us something—such as a trip to the north woods for a vacation, and also to Chicago where Circus had sung on the radio. He actually acted like he thought it was fun to give away his money where it would do a boy or somebody a lot of good; he enjoyed it as much as the Sugar Creek Gang enjoyed swimming and diving in Sugar Creek.

Then, without even having time to think straight, I felt very queer on the inside 'cause I remembered the kind old man had once hinted to us that he might send the whole gang down to Palm Tree Island for a vacation just to see what it was like to be in a foreign country.

Before the old man read the letter carefully, he just glanced at it. Then he took off his glasses and wiped his eyes with his red bandana handkerchief, like the kind Dragonfly's dad always used, 'cause he was always sneezing like Dragonfly was and had to have a large handkerchief. Nearly all the Sugar Creek Gang's dads used large handkerchiefs because all of our fathers were farmers. And nearly all farmers used that kind of handkerchief, sometimes tying them around their necks for dusters to keep the dust out.

The old man laid his glasses down on the table beside his black Bible which was open there like he had been reading it, which he was always doing. He had several other very important-looking books there too, which the gang knew helped explain some hard things in the Bible. The old man would rather read something like that than anything else.

Well, the next thing I knew he had handed the

letter to Big Jim and said, "In a minute I want you to read it to us, but first let me tell you a story."

I was always all set for a story when Old Man Paddler was all set to tell one, 'cause he could tell better stories better than anybody I knew. So all of us got ready to listen, and it was a very good story. There was a mystery in it and everything which, as soon as the old man had finished, I knew was going to get all tangled up with the Sugar Creek Gang.

". . . so, boys," he finished, "that's the end of the story. It's a sad ending. I've never known what happened to my twin brother."

Old Man Paddler looked across to the wall to the map of Palm Tree Island which hung there, and he had a faraway expression in his eyes like he was seeing his brother again, and maybe in his memory was playing with him again in and out of Sugar Creek and all around these same hills where our gang had its good times now.

Little Jim was sitting beside me and was leaning up against my right arm, and Poetry was chewing gum hard, and all of us felt kind of sad. Then the old man said, "Boys—"

What he told us then almost made the cold chills run up and down my spine. He said, "Last night I dreamed my twin brother was alive and that he was down on Palm Tree Island, needing somebody to help him get away from something. It seemed like in my dream that he didn't have very long to live and also it seemed like he wasn't saved and wouldn't get to go to heaven. I could see him down there, lonesome and sick and calling for me to help him, and I couldn't 'cause I couldn't move—"

The old man stopped, sighed, opened the top of his cookstove, picked up an iron poker, and stirred up the fire. After he picked up the teakettle and poured boiling water on some sassafras roots which he had just put into a small clean pan on the stove, he sat down again and said, "All right, Big Jim, read the letter to us." Big Jim did, and a part of the letter which was from a missionary, was:

> Thank you again for the check. It is so thoughtful of you to remember us in this way. We can now buy the refrigerator and thus save many dollars worth of food; also we can enjoy the luxury of a cold drink now and then. It makes me think of what the Lord Jesus said once about giving a cup of *cold* water in His Name and getting a reward for it. May the Lord Himself give you a generous reward for your kindness to us, His missionaries. We shall be glad to know more about you and how you happened to know of our need here.
>
> We occasionally have guests from the

United States, and if you ever happen down this way, we shall be pleased to entertain you. Palm Tree Island, as you know, is a very close neighbor to the United States, being only a ninety-minute trip by air from Miami, Florida. . . .

When Big Jim read that, I felt even more excited, and I just sort of knew something was going to happen to make the whole gang very happy.

Big Jim finished the letter, and all of us were very quiet for a jiffy. Then the old man sighed heavily and acted like he was ready to change the subject. He looked across at the map again and said something kind of low like he hadn't meant for us to hear it but was speaking to Somebody else who was in the room. What he said was: "And if he is alive, and needs help, please show us what to do."

The old man stood again, pushed his Bible back to the other side of the table against the wall, and got busy finishing the sassafras tea. Dragonfly said in my ear, "Sounded like he was praying. Why didn't he bow his head and shut his eyes?"

And Little Jim, who had heard Dragonfly say that and was a very smart little guy, and was always saying things like that anyway, said, "He and God are good friends. Besides, maybe he bowed his soul anyway." Then, just as if he hadn't said anything important, Little Jim shuffled to his feet and scrambled over to the stairway where Big Jim was sitting on the bottom step and squeezed in between him and the log wall of the house.

Right away we had our tea party and pretty soon after that we were all on our way home again, each one of us talking about what if we got to go to Palm Tree Island and, if we did, wishing we could go in the wintertime while it was so cold along Sugar Creek. We were also wishing it was warm enough right that minute to go in swimming, which it certainly wasn't. As soon as we got out of the cave, we walked along through the snow, which was blowing and drifting. I looked out across old Sugar Creek's sad and frozen and very white face and wished I was on Palm Tree Island right that minute, swimming in a creek down there where it was warm. I was wondering as I waded along in the snow beside Poetry and the rest of the gang, if we would really get to go.

"If we do," Poetry said to me in his voice which was half boy's and half man's, "I'm going to look for Old Man Paddler's twin brother. Say, I'll bet you something important."

Poetry stopped, pulled one glove off for a jiffy and held one fat forefinger up to his lips and said mysteriously, "Something very, *very* important."

"What?" I said.

25

He said, "I'll bet if we get to go we'll *find* Old Man Paddler's twin brother and bring him back with us."

Poetry caught my arm a minute and stopped me and pulled me back behind a big maple tree, and said, "Promise me something, Bill Collins."

The wind was blowing terribly hard on that side of the tree, so I said, "Sure, hurry up. I'm cold."

"Promise me that you and I will find the old man's brother."

"He's dead," I said.

"How do you know?"

" 'Cause," I said, "if he was alive he would have come home a long time ago." That sounded like good sense, and after I'd said it I was proud of myself for having thought of it.

"Promise me!" he demanded gruffly.

I said, "All right, but I don't believe it." I really didn't, although I was already beginning to half hope Poetry might be right.

As I turned in at our gate, my heart was pounding hard 'cause I was going to ask my parents right away if I could go with the gang to Palm Tree Island if they went.

4

Boy oh boy! Just like we had done that time we were on our airplane trip to Chicago, so we did it again—went zooming up through the middle of the sky. Only instead of there being trees and little old, twisting, winding Sugar Creek down below us, there was the Atlantic Ocean and the Gulf Stream and the long, rough-and-tumble-looking, brown-colored islands called the Florida Keys, which are coral and limestone islands. From our airplane they looked like the skeleton of some great big ugly dinosaur, with his backbone all disjointed, lying down there in the middle of the ocean.

I was sitting right beside a little window, with Dragonfly sitting beside me. He was holding onto a paper bag which was for him to put his breakfast in just in case he didn't want it, like he didn't that time we all went to Chicago. But Dragonfly was feeling fine this time, and so were all the rest of us, as we roared along through and over and under the whitest clouds I had ever seen, with clear sky all around also.

"I certainly hope I don't get asthma," Dragonfly said, remembering he had gotten it up in the airplane the other time and also remembering that had been one of the reasons why his parents had been slow to make up their minds to let him go. They thought there might be too many flowers on the island, and he might be allergic to some of them and not be able to breathe, and then our whole trip would be spoiled. Dragonfly's parents were always worrying about something anyway, and his mother was especially afraid of black cats running across the road in front of us.

"Anyway," Dragonfly said, grinning, "there won't be any black cats up here in the sky and running across this sky road."

Little Jim piped across the aisle to us, "It's a pretty road. I wonder how much farther it is up to heaven."

Right away my thoughts were flying in an airplane of their own. I was wondering if maybe heaven was away up there somewhere on some planet or other, and if it was maybe the prettiest place God had ever made, and if there would be a lot of surprises for everybody who got to go there. Maybe He hadn't told us very much about heaven in the Bible because it was kind of like Christmas

28

presents my Mom buys for me. Mom doesn't tell me what I'm going to get so I'll have something to be surprised about when Christmas really comes. I got to thinking, what if the whole Sugar Creek Gang could go to heaven at the same time like we were going to Palm Tree Island right that minute, and what if Old Man Paddler had paid for us all so we could go and could get in free and everything?

And do you know, I happened to think of something very important, which I asked Little Jim about the very first time I had a chance, and he said it was right. And that was, that just as Old Man Paddler had paid for us all to go to Palm Tree Island, so Somebody had already paid for all it costs to take anybody to heaven. And He didn't pay it with money either, but with His blood which He gave for everybody one day when He was hanging on a cross and died there.

But my thoughts didn't get to think very far 'cause all of a sudden Dragonfly beside me began to feel very sick. I knew he was going to lose his breakfast and everything else he had eaten since breakfast, such as two candy bars.

"Quick," I said, "let's go into the washroom. You might have too much breakfast for that little paper bag!" In a jiffy both of us slipped out of our seats and hurried back to the tail of the plane and through a small door into a little room which had a wash basin and running water, just like the plane we'd been on before had had. The minute Dragon-fly and I got in there he swayed like he was dizzy and held onto me and I onto him, and just as quick as that it was all over—

Well, pretty soon—in fact, right away—the stewardess came in too. Right away I went out and sat down and waited for Dragonfly to come back, which he did after a while, grinning and feeling fine again, and we were all happy.

"What if we find Old Man Paddler's brother?" I said to Poetry, who was sitting in one of the nice, big, soft-cushioned seats right in front of me.

He said, "We're going to!"

"How do you know?" I said.

He said, "I don't know how I know, but I know I know."

I hoped that what he knew he knew was true.

Just as we were about to fly past the Florida Keys, Little Jim seemed to notice them for the first time. He said, "What are those big brown things down there in the water?"

Circus told him, "The Florida Keys. We use them to unlock the Gulf of Mexico."

Poetry spoke up and said, "How'd you like to have a piano that big, and be a giant and play on it?"

Little Jim grinned and kept still, and I noticed

that his fingers on his knees were moving like he was playing his mom's piano back in Sugar Creek.

Well, in just exactly ninety minutes we began to get close to Palm Tree Island. I looked out and very far down and saw the blue ocean, and it looked just like some of the pretty blue velvet in my mom's sewing room at Sugar Creek. It had a lot of little wrinkles in it, only I knew the wrinkles were great big waves maybe ten feet high.

The next thing we knew we had landed. And all of us, one at a time, were climbing down the little portable stairway out of the plane to the ground, and we were on Palm Tree Island. All kinds of people were away up high on a balcony of the airport looking down at us and waving to different people coming off the plane, and everybody was talking Spanish and everybody was smiling and happy. Everybody looked like they thought we were the most wonderful people in the world and that we were their best friends.

I won't even take time to tell you about going through what they call the "routine of customs" 'cause Barry Boyland, who had come with us and was supposed to be taking care of us, took care of that for us. Pretty soon we were in two taxicabs that looked like they had been made in America, and all of us were out on a very pretty wide, paved road, driving as fast as we could toward Palacia.

The prettiest great big royal palm trees were all along the roadside, and all kinds of other trees and so many flowers of all colors, especially red and pink and also all kinds of other colors and all the different-looking buildings and houses with children looking out of the windows, which had iron or copper or brass bars instead of glass.

I looked at Dragonfly and he was looking worried.

"Look at the flowers," I said.

He shut his eyes and said, "I'll bet I'm allergic. I won't look at them."

"Goose!" Poetry said beside him. "You don't get allergic to flowers with your *eyes* but with your *nose!*" Dragonfly laughed 'cause it was funny; then he sneezed, which wasn't funny, and I knew he was going to have trouble.

Well, if there is anything in the world I would rather do than anything else, unless it's swimming and diving in Sugar Creek, it's going to a circus where there are hundreds and hundreds of people. And everybody is talking and walking up and down, and everywhere people are trying to sell you something you don't need. Voices are calling and people are laughing. Everybody is all dressed up and happy, and nobody looks like anybody else; and you have plenty of money in your pocket and can buy what you want to if you want to.

Well, that's what I first thought of when we got out of our taxi on the prettiest and biggest street in Palacia which is called the Prado, which I think means "parade." They were having some kind of a celebration or something, I think, and I never saw so many different kinds of different-looking people. And boy oh boy, it was so warm that winter day it was actually hot!

For a minute, though, I couldn't tell which end my head was on because of all the noise of people's voices calling, and other people tugging at my elbows and trying to sell me something. It seemed that all the people in the world were swarming around me like bees out of one of Dad's beehives back home, and they were trying to light on me. Everybody was either trying to sell us something or to get us to decide to go to their hotel to stay, or to do something I couldn't tell what. Also nearly everybody was trying to sell something which looked like United States government bonds or something.

Dragonfly, at my side, exclaimed to me above the roar of the noise all around us, "What in the world are they trying to sell us?"

And Poetry, who had studied about Palm Tree Island in a library book, said, "Lottery tickets," which is what they were.

Pretty soon whatever Barry had had to do at the

place wherever we were was done, and we all got back into our taxicabs and rode to a hotel which was right across the street from a great big beautiful capitol building which looked even prettier than the pictures of the Capitol of the United States at Washington, D. C. Right away Poetry started to quote a poem which goes:

> My country, 'tis of thee,
> Sweet land of liberty.

Circus started to sing it. Then we all went bashfully inside the hotel, which had an open front, which means we didn't have to go through any doors of any kind but could just walk right straight in.

Well, I certainly didn't have any idea that almost right away after we'd been in Palacia awhile, that Poetry and I were going to get lost like we did on another trip—the one we took up into the north woods in the United States. There really wasn't any sense in our getting lost either, but what can you do if you *are* lost except wish you weren't and try to get unlost again?

This is the way it happened. We had all gone up to our very high-ceilinged hotel rooms and left our luggage and were down again in the street. We were supposed to be going to a café somewhere where we could all eat. Dragonfly was especially hungry because he had not had a chance to digest the last food he had eaten.

As I told you before, there were so many people that it was almost as crowded as walking through the terribly tall weeds that grow down along the swamp along Sugar Creek.

Pretty soon we were maybe ten or more blocks from the hotel and Poetry and I were standing still for a jiffy looking into a shop window at some very pretty tooled-leather billfolds, and I was wishing I could buy one for me and another for my dad.

We all were walking on when all of a sudden Poetry, who was with me alone again, grabbed me by the arm and stopped me so quick I was bumped into by maybe three people who were walking close behind me. The rest of the gang was ahead of us with all kinds of people between us chattering and making a lot of noise.

In fact, Poetry and I had stopped and were look-ing into a shop window where there were some very pretty bookends made out of mahogany wood. There were round mahogany balls the size of cro-quet balls fastened on the outside of each one, with a little wooden handle on each ball, like the kind people used to beat tom-toms—the kind of drums used by people on Palm Tree Island. In my mind for just a half jiffy I was thinking of my folks and of our living room at home. And I could see my father, who would be sitting beside our heating stove, turn halfway around and reach over to our library table and take out a book from between those very pretty bookends. And then he would say to my grayish-brown-haired Mom, who would have Charlotte Ann in her lap sleeping, "These are surely very pretty bookends our Bill bought for us while he was down in the West Indies. Just think— he flew down there by airplane!"

Right there my thoughts were interrupted by Poetry grabbing my arm and hissing, "Hey! Look." He whirled me around and I looked, and would you believe it? It was a great big brown billy goat with harness on just like the kind of harness my dad uses on our horses back along Sugar Creek.

The goat was hitched up to a little vehicle about the size of a wheelchair, only it had four wheels. Somebody was in the chair, driving and riding and the goat was trotting down the street with all the other traffic. There were cars which were blowing their horns almost all the time, and also buses which were doing the same thing and also people walking and carrying things to sell. It was certainly an interesting sight, seeing that brown billy goat being driven along the street.

Then I gasped and almost jumped out of my shoes which I had to wear because of having to be dressed up. "Look!" I half screamed to Poetry.

"It's Old Man Paddler!" But I knew it wasn't and couldn't have been because that kind old man was in the United States. And yet, sitting up in that little buggy was somebody that looked almost like him, except his whiskers were not so long and were gray instead of white.

Poetry must have thought it *was* Old Man Paddler, or else he forgot for a minute where we were, for he yelled out to the old man in the buggy, "Hi, there, Mr. Paddler!"

But the old man didn't even look around but kept his eyes right straight on the street ahead and his goat trotted right on and turned a corner and disappeared.

All of a sudden I remembered Old Man Paddler's lost twin brother and a funny feeling jumped right up from inside me somewhere. The next thing I knew I was off down the street on the run after the goat. I swung around a corner lickety-sizzle and so fast and in such a blind hurry that I bumped into several people. Then I got all mixed up with the crowds of people which were swarming everywhere, and I didn't know where I was.

Whatever makes a boy do such crazy things and, as my mom says, be so impulsive—which means doing things quick whenever you want to without stopping to think first—I say, whatever makes a boy do things like I did right that minute, I don't know.

But I had already done it and when I sort of came to my senses, which I was supposed to have, I looked every which way and all I could see was people and people and more people and narrow sidewalks. Everybody was trying to sell something or to ask for something, and everybody was talking Spanish fast to everybody else. Cars were honking and streetcars were going past and omnibuses were doing the same thing, and I didn't see anybody I knew.

Everywhere I looked, everything and everybody looked like everything and everybody else. I remembered the time last year when Poetry and I had been lost and didn't know where we were, away up in the north woods. Every tree had looked like every other tree, and every direction had looked like every other direction.

I was standing right in front of an open-front store which looked like a meat market. Only there weren't any refrigerators, but the hams and shoulders and steaks and dressed chickens were hanging right out in the open air. The first thing I thought of without trying to think was that there weren't any flies swarming around the meat, which there would have been if it had been in the United States. All around me, too, were boys and men with little portable boxes and trays with unwrapped candy and cakes and cookies on them. They were

38

trying to sell them to people, and there weren't any flies on the food either. And without intending to, I thought Palm Tree Island was a nice place. But then I remembered that I was lost and I began to be actually scared. I was not used to being in big cities 'cause in the United States I lived in the country; so I felt very bashful and half scared.

All of a sudden I heard a voice beside me that was like an angel's voice 'cause it was Poetry's.

"Boy oh boy!" he puffed, which showed he had been running from somewhere. "Am I glad to see you! I thought I was lost!"

"You are," I said. "We both are."

"*What!*" he exclaimed.

"I ran after the old man in the wheelchair and the goat and got lost," I said.

And he said the same thing, and we were both lost. Everywhere we looked everything and everybody still looked like everything and everybody else.

Just that minute I heard a voice beside me and it was saying in English, "Give me one cent. Give me one cent."

I looked down and it was a very pretty little girl with black, kind of kinky hair and kind of sad eyes and poor clothes and a thin face, and she was holding out one small hand to us and waiting for me or Poetry to give her a penny.

It's a queer feeling, having somebody beg for a penny when they look hungry, and it was also a surprise for me to hear her talk English. So I said, "Sure, I'll give you something," and I took out a whole dollar and gave it to her and said, "Can you tell me where I am? Where is the Gran America Hotel?" which was the name of the hotel where we were staying.

But do you know, she just shook her head and started talking some kind of Spanish. Right away there were about seven other children around us, and also walking merchants who were trying to beg or to sell us something.

"The only English she knows," Poetry said, "is 'Give me one cent,'" and I believed it.

Well, Poetry had a bright idea. He said, "We don't have to stay lost. All we have to do is to get a taxicab and have the driver take us to Gran America Hotel, and if we wait long enough Barry and the rest of the gang will be there, and we'll be all right."

It was a good idea, and we'd have done that instead of the crazy thing we did do, if we'd had enough money between us to pay for the taxi. But for some reason neither one of us did have, because we had left most of our money with Barry so we wouldn't lose it.

"I've got only five cents," Poetry said.

"I said, "I've got a dollar—what!"

Of course, I didn't have any dollar, because I'd wanted to feel big by giving it all to the kind of pretty girl, and also because I had felt sorry for her. I didn't have more than fifteen cents. Well, we had been in taxis in Chicago, and we knew we maybe couldn't go very far for twenty cents and maybe cabs were much higher in Palacia than in Chicago, we thought. So we stood there kind of going around in circles to get away from everybody who was trying to sell us something. Then Poetry said, "I know where the hotel is. Let's go down this way. That's south, isn't it? Remember we came straight north when we left the hotel? Well, now if we go south we're all right. We'll come to the capitol and then we'll know where we are."

"Which way is south?" I asked him, and he grinned, feeling much better, and we both remembered that we'd had a lot of fun once finding south the way Boy Scouts do, with a watch and a match or stick.

We certainly couldn't tell which way south was by the sun 'cause it was almost noon and the sun was almost straight overhead, 'cause we were much closer to the equator down there than we were up in northern Minnesota that time and so we *had* to use the watch.

Pretty soon Poetry had his watch out, and was holding it flat in the palm of his fat hand.

"Here," I said, "here's a match," picking one up off the sidewalk and handing it to him.

In a jiffy Poetry was standing the little stick straight up at the circumference of the watch and was also twisting the watch around a little so the shadow made by the match would fall straight along the hour hand of the watch.

"Now," Poetry said in a businesslike voice, "straight south will be just halfway between the shadow of the match and the twelve on the dial," which is the way I remembered was the way to find south.

Say, south was a long way south of where I thought it was. Anyway, we knew which way to go if we wanted to get to the capitol building, so we dodged around among the people, not stopping to look anybody in the eye 'cause every time we did, whoever it was—or nearly whoever it was—would try to sell us a candy bar or a lottery ticket or a string of beads or something.

It's fun being lost if you don't think you really are, or if you think you won't be lost very long. But say, the farther we walked the more every street corner looked like every other corner and the sun was pouring down hot on us and we also were beginning to get hungry. Pretty soon we stopped and looked into each other's worried eyes and said to each other at the same time, "We're lost again!"

5

LOST AND BROKE and hungry are three funny feelings, and we had all three of them.

"Say," Poetry said, "let's ask a policeman where to find the capitol building," which is the first thing a lost boy ought to do anyway if he's lost in a city—ask a policeman. I had never seen so many policemen in my life as there seemed to be on the streets of Palacia, each one carrying a revolver in a holster at his side.

So I picked out the nearest one who was standing right beside a very pretty candy stand, and said to him, "Say, mister, can you tell us where to find the capitol?"

He looked down at me and grinned cheerfully and said, *"El Capitolio?"* He hesitated, looked at me very carefully, and must have wondered what made my hair so red and my freckles so many and the rest of me so ordinary-looking. Then he started to explain in Spanish which sounded like a lot of pretty American words all tangled up and spoken backward and upside-down and—well, that was that; we didn't get any help there.

Besides, he had to leave us 'cause the corner where we were had a traffic jam right that minute because a long bus was trying to turn it. The street was so narrow and the tall buildings were so close together that the bus had to stop and back up, and go forward and stop and back up and go forward again before it could keep on going.

All of a sudden ɪ had a bright idea. I said, "Why don't we get on that bus and ride? I've got enough money for a bus fare."

"But it's going *east,*" he said.

"It is not," I said. "It's going south," which it was, but Poetry said it wasn't and maybe it wasn't. Anyway, before we could decide which way it was going it was gone.

But it was an idea anyway, so pretty soon when a streetcar came along we got on and sat down. It was just like a small Chicago streetcar, with different kinds of people on it—Palm Tree Islanders, with their dark faces and their very black and kind of kinky hair, and very pretty dark eyes, especially the girls and women; Negroes with interesting hair, and with their thicker lips than the Palm Tree Islanders; also, there were Chinese on the car. All the people were dressed just like American people, and the ones that were talking were talking Spanish or something that sounded like it.

"Look!" I said to Poetry. "We're turning, we're going—we're going in another direction!" which we were.

"I wish I could speak Spanish," I said. "I'm going to study it when I get into high school."

"Hey!" Poetry said all of a sudden. "Look! There goes that billy goat again!"

And sure enough, there it was, and the old man with the long whiskers was driving along, sitting like a king on a moving throne, with the goat trotting very obediently ahead.

"Did you *ever* see anybody look so much like Old Man Paddler in your life?" Poetry said.

I said, "I never did." I just knew it was Old Man Paddler's brother.

For maybe about a minute we saw the goat, and then it was gone, 'cause a streetcar and a goat wouldn't both have room enough to go side by side on a narrow Palacia street. Anyway, the goat turned out into another street which I noticed was wider, in fact, very wide for a change, and it was a boulevard which ran beside Palacia Bay.

"That's El Torro Castle," Poetry said. "Right over there on the other side of the harbor."

"I've read stories about El Torro Castle," I said.

They were terrible stories of young men who had rebelled against the government a long time ago and they had been taken to Torro Castle and put in a dungeon or a torture chamber. And then, if they didn't do or say what they were supposed to, they were taken to another place in the castle, cut in pieces and thrown down through a hole into the water below and were eaten by sharks. Sharks are very large, always hungry fish with small sharp teeth, and they like to eat people.

But we didn't have time to tell any fish stories just then 'cause Poetry nudged me quick and said, "Hey, this isn't where we want to go! Look! The old man is stopping."

Well, I remembered Old Man Paddler, and in my mind's eye I could see tears in his eyes as he said, "Boys, it's the one wish of my life before I die—to see my brother again."

It just seemed like Poetry and I had to do something. So we were out of our cane-backed seat in a jiffy and lurching our way to the end of the car to get out as soon as it stopped. The very minute it did stop we were out, and going right straight over to the old man.

Well, we knew a few Spanish words, such as *"Buenas dias,"* for "Good day"; *"Buenas tardes,"* for "Good afternoon"; *"Buenas noches,"* for "Good night." So we hurried over to the breakwater, which was a wall made of cement to break the force of the water of the bay and to keep it from getting up onto the boulevard. There the old man had stopped, and was sitting and looking out across the bay toward the lighthouse.

Poetry, as you maybe already know, wasn't a very bashful boy except in church, and that was only because his voice was changing and sometimes sounded like a duck with a bad cold. Anyway, both of us went right up beside the small wheelchair-sized buggy which had tires like bicycle tires, and the goat acted like a lamb, and Poetry said, *"Buenas tardes,* Mr. Paddler."

Saying that reminded me that it was afternoon but *not* after *dinner,* 'cause I hadn't had any dinner and was terribly hungry. Even thinking about sharks eating somebody had made me hungry.

That old man turned from looking out across the bay and looked down at us and he had the same kind eyes Old Man Paddler had. And he looked like him except for his whiskers which were more gray than white and he had a scar on his forehead that started at just above his right eyebrow and ran right up into the place where his hat covered his hair. He was wearing a clean hat that looked like Dad's Sunday straw hat back at Sugar Creek.

Then the old man smiled at us and said, *"Buenas*

tardes." He said something else in Spanish, which of course we couldn't understand.

Well, I knew that if he was an American he could speak English, so I said to him, "Good afternoon, Mr. Paddler."

And he said surprised like, "Good afternoon; it is a beautiful day." Then he looked puzzled. "You speak English?"

"Sure," I said. "We are Americans. We flew down on a plane." It felt good to say that—as if I was even more important than I am.

"Many Americans come to Palacia in the wintertime," the old man replied. "They think Billy and I are quite a curiosity. You have goats in America?" he asked, and then he sort of looked away out across the bay toward the El Torro Castle and said, "See that old castle with the black cannon rusting up on the top there? That's where I was born—up there in a cell."

What? I thought. *That's a crazy place to be born.*

Then the old man turned around and looked at me and I was so startled I gasped out loud, he looked so much like Old Man Paddler. I felt even more woozy in the head when he said, "Yes, boys, I was a full-grown man when I was born, never knew what it was to be a boy like you; never knew what it was to romp and play and swim and dive

49

and do things like other boys. I was born right up there." He stopped talking and gestured toward the lighthouse.

And while his face was turned away and while an omnibus was whizzing past right that minute and making a lot of noise, Poetry whispered in my ear and said, "He's crazy."

"He's mentally ill," I whispered back into Poetry's ear, remembering something I'd read in a magazine that people who are like that are supposed to be called "mentally ill" rather than "crazy."

"See that little gondola out there," the old man said. "I used to be an oarsman for one of them—rowed people back and forth every day to visit El Torro Castle. I didn't even have to learn to row—knew how to handle oars as well as any of those old tars out there."

The old man's voice was kind of raspy, like it had talked so much all his life that it had worn out the edges, and a lot of his breath came through with his words, making it sound like he was sighing as well as talking, which maybe he was.

My eyes followed his out across the pretty blue water of Palacia Bay where there were a half-dozen boats. They had canvas tops on them and looked like pictures I'd seen of covered wagons which used to cross the prairies of the United States. Only now the sides of the canvas tops were rolled up, and you could see the people who were being rowed around in the bay.

I wished I could have a ride in one of the taxi boats but I still remembered I was lost, or supposed to be—and also I was trying to find out if the mentally ill old man sitting there like a king in his little vehicle was Old Man Paddler's twin brother. And if he was, what could we do about it? One thing for sure, he sounded like a very sensible crazy man.

"Say, mister, is your name Paddler? Kenneth Paddler?"

He looked around quick like he wanted to see who I was talking to, and when he didn't see anybody he said, "Were you addressing me, sir?"

I was and said so, and he said, "My name is John Machete. That's another thing. When I was born, a full-grown man, I didn't have anybody to name me, so I named myself. See? I named myself after this—" He reached down and pulled out of the seat beside him a long machete, which is a big knife which Palm Tree Island farmers use for cutting sugar cane and for other things, and slipped it out of its tooled-leather sheath.

"Whew!" Poetry whistled. "Look at that, would you?"

I was already looking at the beautiful, shining knife with its gold-inlaid handle.

"It's pretty," I said, and wished I had one for myself to take back home to my dad and for everybody in Sugar Creek to see.

"Yes sir, boys, when I was born a full-grown man, I found this lying right under me. Maybe I never was born, though. Maybe I just came right down out of the sky or somewhere, and this machete belonged to some god or goddess. Maybe I'm a god myself, I don't know."

I started to feel very queer inside. The man was really—well, he was *crazy*, I thought. I grabbed Poetry by the arm and said, "Let's get going. We've got to get back to the hotel. I'm getting hungrier and hungrier."

"You're hungry?" the old man said. And then, because the goat seemed to be hungry also and was trying to nibble on the stone breakwater near which he was standing, the old man scolded him, jerked on one of the lines and said something rough in Spanish, and then he said, "Where do you boys want to go?"

"We're looking for Gran America Hotel," Poetry said.

"Gran America!" the old man asked.

I said, "Yes, it's near the capitol building."

"*El Capitolio* is at the other end of the Prado—here, you go—"

Well, all of a sudden the goat wanted to go and the old man seemed to have the same idea, so he told us just how many blocks to walk till we got to the Prado, which is Palacia's very wide and beautiful boulevard, and if we would walk far enough up the Prado we would find the capitol.

Then the old man clucked to his goat and in a jiffy would have been gone if Poetry hadn't stopped him. "Where do you live, Mr.—Mr.—Machete!"

The old man's voice changed at that, and he said, grumpily, "No one cares where I live. *Buenas tardes*."

He clucked to the goat again and this time he really would have been gone.

But I was so sure he was Kenneth Paddler, Old Man Paddler's twin brother, that I stopped him again, saying, "Wait! We have to know where you live. I—it's very important!"

But he wouldn't stay stopped. Instead, he picked up his machete, and waved it in the air, kind of shook it like he was angry at somebody and then he shoved it back into its leather scabbard. And his goat went trotting down the boulevard, leaving me and Poetry all flabbergasted and disappointed. But we made up our minds to find out who the crazy old geezer was—unless we were both crazy ourselves, or else I was having a dream and pretty soon would wake up and still be in America.

Poetry and I stood there, looking at the flying wheels of the vehicle and the flying heels of the trotting goat and then we looked at each other and said, "Do you suppose all this isn't so? Are we on Palm Tree Island or in America, and are we just dreaming?"

"We're either dreaming or crazy," Poetry said. "Whoever he is, he would make a good Santa Claus for some department store in the United States." That reminded him of a poem about Christmas, which he started to quote:

> 'Twas the night before Christmas,
>   When all through the house,
> Not a creature was stirring
>   Not even a mouse.

Well, there wasn't anything we could do, 'cause we were both broke and lost and it seemed more important right that minute that we get back to the rest of the gang. So we walked along the break-water till we came to a very wide, pretty boulevard, and it was the Prado. We turned into it and started to walk in the only direction there was left to walk, which Poetry said was north and which I said was east. But we didn't bother to find out what direction it was, but kept on going, hoping that pretty soon we would come to the *Capitolio* and then to the hotel and maybe the gang would find us there before long. Boy, was I hungry!

6

TALK ABOUT A PRETTY STREET. I never saw such a
pretty one in my whole life. The sidewalk was right
in the center of it and·Poetry and I walked along
on its marble floor in the shade of very pretty green
trees which we'd already learned were laurel. I
couldn't help but wish they had been in full bloom,
which they are at certain times of the year, then it
would have been just like walking under an arch-
way of pink blossoms.

I was not only hungry, I was also hot, as was
Poetry. He was puffing along beside me and both
of us were sweating harder than if it had been
summertime at Sugar Creek and we were hoeing
potatoes or something. Pretty soon Poetry said,
"Let's rest. I'm tired."

We plopped ourselves down on one of the marble benches which were all along the Prado, on
each side of the center walk, and watched the traffic
going past. On one side of us it was going one way,

and on the other it was going the other; and the traffic was different makes of cars, looking like they had been made in America, bicycles and omnibuses; and every car was blowing its horn too many times too loud. And all around us and in front of us were people and still more people 'cause, as I've already told you, Palacia seemed to be having a celebration of some kind.

We hadn't been seated there more than a half jiffy when a little barefoot boy came along, holding up a string of macaroni beads for sale and talking Spanish. He grinned and his snow-white teeth were as even as two rows of pearls.

"I'm broke," I said to the boy, and shook my head, and Poetry said and did the same thing. But the little barefoot boy kept on pestering us to buy until we got up and went on, saying "No" several times to maybe two dozen people who wanted to sell us something, such as unwrapped candy bars or some cookies or fruit or lottery tickets, or something else.

It would have been fun though if we hadn't still felt lost, and also felt foolish for having chased a billy goat and an old man with whiskers.

"We acted like two crazy fish," Poetry said to me, "running after an old man with whiskers. Look! There's another old man with whiskers just as long as the one we just chased."

I looked and sure enough, sitting on a bench on the other side of the center sidewalk was an old man with whiskers as long as Old Man Paddler's. He had a big white bandage tied all around his head, and looked like he wasn't glad to be alive. All of a sudden I wished I was already grownup and was a doctor, and I even wished I would be a missionary doctor, instead of one in the United States where there were plenty for everybody who was sick.

Well, the closer we got to the *Capitolio,* which we could see after a while, the more sheepish we felt for having chased an old man driving a billy goat with long whiskers. So we made up our minds not to tell the gang.

"They'll think we're just plain cuckoo," Poetry said, and maybe we were, I thought.

Almost right away we passed the *Capitolio,* and were inside the lobby of the hotel and, also almost right away, we saw the gang coming in.

The minute they spied us, Dragonfly let out a half yell and said, "There they are!" He came swishing across the marble floor, past the winding stairway, also past the desk where a big man with a cigar in his mouth sat, and also a big potted palm in the center of the lobby where Poetry and I sat rocking in mahogany rocking chairs near a piano. Right away the gang was all there, asking questions and telling us different things, and everybody was feeling fine with nobody paying much attention to what anybody was saying because we were glad we were all there and all right.

Dragonfly was breathing easy just like he wasn't going to be allergic to Palm Tree Island at all, and that made me feel fine.

"Were you lost?" Dragonfly wanted to know.

"*LOST!*" Poetry and I both exclaimed at the same time in a disgusted tone of voice. We decided to act mysterious though, which we did.

Well, Barry Boyland, right after finding us, stopped at the desk beside the man with the big black cigar, who smiled out of the corner of his mouth where there was room enough to. He phoned the tourist commission and the police headquarters not to look for the lost American boys any longer 'cause they had been found. We really hadn't been, but found ourselves.

We were just ready to go down to a special café, when all of a sudden I heard the most beautiful piano music right behind me. Turning around I saw it was Little Jim sitting at that piano and letting his fingers gallop up and down the keyboard like two race horses, each with five legs, playing some fancy thing which he had memorized back in America. Then we all went out and hurried along behind Barry Boyland and the missionary who had met us at the airport and was acting as our interpreter. The missionary would take what we said in English and translate it for us to whoever we were talking to, and then would translate Spanish back into English for us, so we could talk to anybody we wanted to and be understood.

Pretty soon we were upstairs in an open-air café called *El Aguila*, which means "The Eagle," and were all sitting around two tables covered with white tablecloths, being waited on by a very handsome, dark-skinned young man with a small black moustache. I sat scowling at my menu card which was maybe fifteen inches long, and was yellow and had a lot of Spanish words on it, such as *Lunch Pescado Soute Meunier, Lunch de Pollo Asado*—and a lot of other things.

"I'll take the fish dinner," Big Jim said, and pointed to the words *Lunch Pescado*.

"How'd you know what that is?" I whispered to to him, since I was sitting beside him.

And he said, "That's easy, if you study Latin. *Piscator* is a Latin word which means a fisherman, and—well, that is how I know. Over half of our English words come from the Latin," Big Jim said, he being maybe the best scholar in the whole Sugar Creek Gang.

We were sitting there, each one of us getting in a few words now and then between the others' words, and also between bites of food, which was certainly good. I had decided to eat *Lunch de Carne Vienesa,* which was Vienna meat-loaf dinner, and was meat loaf, brown gravy, rice, fried bananas, roll and butter. That was the first time I'd ever eaten fried bananas.

"We'll show you a banana plantation," the missionary said, and looked at me with a very friendly twinkle in his eye. I thought that he was just like any ordinary person, who liked boys and who wanted to get the boys of Palm Tree Island to become Christians as well as boys in our own country.

Pretty soon our plates were all empty and we went back to the hotel to take a siesta.

"What's a siesta?" Little Jim wanted to know.

"It's an after-dinner nap," I said, wondering if I was right.

"What? A nap in the daytime? I'm not sleepy," Circus said, and looked disappointed, as if he wondered if the missionary thought we were a bunch of little guys.

"Everybody on Palm Tree Island takes a nap right after the noon meal," the missionary said. "It's the custom here."

We walked back to the hotel and I noticed that some of the great big stores, which didn't have any doors, only chains or ropes or grilled gates across their entrances, had all their counters covered with long dust covers, and nobody was selling anything.

"If we rest in the daytime, we'll have plenty of pep for the rest of the day, I'll bet you," Poetry said, and yawned, and several of us did the same thing.

Well, we were back in our rooms in Gran America pretty soon and Poetry and Dragonfly and I were in our room, where there were three beds. We didn't even have any windows. There were doors instead, which opened inside, and we could step right out onto a little balcony which was protected by iron grillwork about as high as our belts. The doors had wooden shutters on them called venetian blinds, and the ceiling was very high. The floor was of cool, different-colored tile.

We stepped through the open doors and out onto a balcony which was there, and looked across the street to the flat roof of a large building. On the roof of that building, which was a little lower than where we were on the fourth floor, were three great big ugly looking dogs which looked different from any dogs I'd ever seen.

Just then I heard a barking not more than fifteen feet to my left, and I looked across to another balcony, which opened out from somebody else's room in our hotel. And there was Circus, barking and bawling like a hound at the dogs across the street.

As quick as anything those great big ugly hounds on the flat roof roused themselves and let out a lot of long-toned bawls at Circus, and for a minute they barked back and forth at each other across the street. Circus knew all about hounds 'cause his dad kept a lot of them and used them in the wintertime to catch different kinds of animals to make a living for his great big family of almost all girls.

Well, that's about all the interesting things which happened that day. The next morning we had one more strange adventure which was very important and also gave me something to really write home to my parents about. In fact, if it hadn't happened this whole story would have been spoiled.

I could hardly wait until tomorrow 'cause I wanted to get out into what is called the "interior" to see the savages I'd heard so much about. So far I hadn't seen anybody that looked like I thought people ought to look who needed missionaries. I certainly hadn't expected electric lights and radios and everybody dressed up even more than Americans, and I certainly didn't expect the people to be even better looking than the people who lived at Sugar Creek; but most of them were, even the girls and women.

But, here goes for the adventure. It happened because Dragonfly had parents who were superstitious. That little rascal not only believed that a black cat running in front of your path meant bad luck, but he was always believing in things which were supposed to mean *good* luck, too, such as four-leaf clovers, and horseshoes, and things like that. Well, just before we had left Sugar Creek to go to Miami, he had found an old rusty horseshoe under a board in their barn. His mom had hung it up over the entrance to their kitchen and had said to him, "You're going to have some very good luck, Roy. I have been afraid to let you go to Palm Tree Island, but your finding this from our old Topsy horse who died ten years ago means something special, I'm sure."

Dragonfly believed it and was looking for good luck all the time we were there.

"Maybe I won't be allergic to flowers," Dragonfly said, "because of that horseshoe."

"That'll depend on your nose," Poetry said, "not on a ten-year-old rusty horseshoe."

I said the same thing, and Dragonfly grunted and said, "Just you wait and see! Look here—"

I looked and he pulled out of his pocket something that looked like a United States bond of some kind, and it was a lottery ticket. We were in our room at the time and Circus was still barking at the hounds across the street and they were still standing there looking across and up at him savagely and barking back. They would stop now and then and look lazy and disgusted at him for interrupting their sleep, which is what he had done and was still doing.

"Tomorrow this will win at the lottery," Dragonfly said.

"What lottery?" I said.

He said, "Barry is taking us to see how the government makes some of its money at what is called the *loteria*. He told us about that while you were lost yesterday."

"We weren't lost," I said. By that time Poetry and I had made up our minds that we really hadn't been, and we both said so.

In a little while we had breakfast right in the dining room of the hotel itself. We were waited on by a man in a black suit—there not being any girl waitresses in Palacia, except in a very few cafés. Right after breakfast, we all got on a streetcar and went down to what is called the old Treasury Building to the *loteria*. As soon as we got inside, we went into a large room which had in it a table long enough to reach from one end of the room to the other. Behind it, sitting down, were a dozen or more important-looking men with serious faces who looked like the men in a picture I'd seen of the Supreme Court of the United States. In front of each man was a notebook, a lot of papers and pens and other things.

At the edge of the room was another table of about the same length and width, and behind it was another row of important-looking men, each one looking very solemn and what my dad would call "dignified."

"Look!" Dragonfly said. "See those two big worlds!"

I looked and saw two great big balls, one of them as tall in diameter as Dad is tall, and the other about as big in diameter as Little Jim is tall, which is about four feet. Both balls were made out of brass, it looked like, and had a lot of fancy grill-work.

"What do you suppose they've got on the inside of them?" Circus wanted to know.

The missionary who was with us said, "There are thousands of marble-sized balls in each one, and on each marble there is a number. The numbers on the marbles in the large globe represent the numbers on the lottery tickets which are sold all over the island. And the numbers on the marbles in the smaller globe tell how much money each ticket is going to win."

I looked at Dragonfly and he had his hand on the inside of his coat pocket, and I knew that he was holding onto that lottery ticket which he had bought yesterday. I also knew that he was thinking about the rusty horseshoe that was hanging over the kitchen door of their house back in Sugar Creek.

There were all kinds of people there, including some important-looking Americans who were in Palacia for winter vacations.

All of a sudden while we were standing there I saw two big men rush out from somewhere to that great big brass globe and grab it by two handles which were sticking out from behind it in the back. Then, as if they were doing the most important thing in the world, they began to turn that globe over and over and over. Everybody in the room was very quiet, even the Sugar Creek Gang. There were maybe two hundred people there, and nearly everyone of them was holding onto a lottery ticket or a whole bunch of them, watching with eyes that looked like a boy's eyes look in the mirror when he is sick and has a fever.

The globe turned around and around and over and over, and for a minute even my brain went around and around, and I thought, *What if Dragonfly wins?* Pretty soon there was another man, in fact, at the very same time, standing beside the smaller globe and was turning it all by himself. And all the little marbles on the inside of the two globes were rattling and rattling with a roar that made me think of a terrible rainstorm on the shingled roof of our barn back home. Then with-

67

out my hardly having noticed how they got there, I saw two little boys standing at each globe. Quick as a flash two of the boys pulled a lever at each globe and, also as quick as a flash, out tumbled a marble from each globe. Each marble rolled into a long brass trough, tumbled down the whole length of the trough and went kerploppety-plop into a very bright cut-glass bowl like one on my mom's sideboard at home. Then with everybody still keeping still, I heard one of the little boys call out with a very high-pitched voice that sounded like one of the Sugar Creek Gang in swimming, a long number in Spanish. Just as quick as he called it, a little boy beside the smaller globe called out another number.

"What's the long number for?" Dragonfly wanted to know.

The missionary said, "That's the number on the lottery ticket which somebody somewhere has bought."

"Then what's the *little* number for?" Dragonfly wanted to know, and there was a feverish look in his eyes.

"The second number," the missionary said, "tells how much money was earned by the ticket whose number was just called."

Dragonfly's head was ducked a little at that time and I could see that he was looking down on the inside of his pocket to see what his number was. The boys read each number in Spanish and every time one was read in Spanish, Barry, who knew Spanish, would translate for us—just for fun.

Just as quick as the two numbers were called, the two balls were placed side by side on some kind of a board which Barry said must be a reckoning board or something, right in front of the very stern-faced man.

Well, it was a very interesting sight for a while until we got tired of watching and then we were going to see Chinatown. Every time somebody won *something*, although most of the people who were winning were not there, but would probably find it out when the newspaper was printed later on in the day, or else while listening to the radio; and everybody's ticket which wasn't any good would be thrown away.

We were getting ready to leave and go to Chinatown when, all of an excited sudden, Dragonfly gasped like he had been shot just as the little boy at the large globe called out a long number. His nervous voice hissed to me, *"That's my number!"*

Almost before I had a chance to think—in fact, I couldn't I was so excited—I heard the other little boy at the small globe call out, *"Con cien pesos."*

Then I heard Barry say, "One hundred dollars," which was the same number so many of the balls had on them. And I knew Dragonfly had won a hundred dollars!

Boy oh boy! I thought. *One hundred dollars! Dragonfly has won!*

And he had. Instead of being glad though, he was scared and had a terribly scared look on his face.

"What's the matter?" I said to Dragonfly, not even waiting for him to say anything.

He said, "What'll I do with a whole hundred dollars?"

Boy oh boy! I knew what I'd have done with it, I thought. First, I'd buy a whole great big two-pound box of chocolate candy for my mom. Then I'd buy a new pair of skates for Dad and a new sled for my baby sister, Charlotte Ann, and a new tea-kettle for Old Man Paddler to use to make sassafras tea for the Sugar Creek Gang when we came up to see him. I might even buy a new baseball glove for Dad who didn't have any and always had to use my old one all the time whenever he and I played together.

I didn't even have time to finish thinking about what I'd do with a hundred dollars, 'cause right that minute I heard the missionary say to Barry, "That's something our new Christians give up for Christ—gambling with the lottery. All these old sins just drop off the new Christians like snow melts off the roof back in the United States when there is a fire in the house."

Dragonfly heard him say that, and so also did different ones of the rest of us, and so Dragonfly was afraid to let anybody know he had a winning ticket. He sidled over to me and said, in a kind of low voice, "I don't see why it's wrong. I'm going to get the hundred dollars anyway!"

"Like fun," Poetry said, who had heard him say what he had said, and about that time we all had it decided for us that it was time to go someplace else, to Chinatown first and later to get on an omnibus and go out into the country to the mission farm, where there was an old swimming hole and where the gang was going in swimming. Palm Tree Island was certainly a very warm country even in the wintertime.

"Might as well tear it up," I whispered to Dragonfly as we were on our way out of the old Treasury Building. He stopped, looked at me with his dragonflylike eyes and said, "I certainly will not. I'm going to keep it for a souvenir, going to paste it into a book when I get home—in fact, I'm going to put it in a picture frame on the wall of my room and it'll always mean good luck in my life, I'll bet you. Say, when my Mom sees that—!"

"It won't mean good luck," I said. "It'll mean bad luck—like it does today."

71

"It will not," Dragonfly said, and he began to get a very stubborn look on his face and I knew he wouldn't change his mind, so I said, "All right, then. Forget it."

"I won't even do that," he said. "It's a souvenir."

Anyway, it was that old lottery ticket which had a lot to do with getting us into another escapade out on the mission farm and which shoved us all of a sudden into one of the most interesting and exciting experiences that could ever happen to a boy.

7

WE DIDN'T STAY VERY LONG in Chinatown, only long enough to notice that the very interesting-looking Chinese looked just like the Chinese did in the Chicago Chinatown we'd all been in the year before. Little Jim nudged me once when we were waiting for the missionary and Barry to get through talking to a Chinese storekeeper, and said to me, "I wonder if there are any missionaries down here from America who are having any Sunday school for the Chinese boys and girls."

"I don't know," I said, and afterward we found out there were thousands and thousands of pretty little Chinese boys and girls who not only didn't go to any Sunday school, but didn't have any Sunday school to go to.

When we found out, I looked down at Little Jim and he had his fists doubled up, and for a minute he had an expression on his face like he had once in a gang fight on Bumblebee Hill back in the United States.

"What's the matter?" I said to him.

He said, "I'm mad!"

"Why?" I said.

He said, like he was just ready to sock somebody, and there were tears in his voice, "Why doesn't somebody come down here and start a Chinese Sunday school?"

A little later, when we were all on our way back to the hotel, Little Jim was still looking angry, only he looked sad too, and he said to me something kind of strange. And it was, "How old do you have to be to be a missionary?"

I didn't get a chance to answer him, but I knew he was thinking something very important, like he always is.

Well, we enjoyed the omnibus ride of about a half hour out to the mission, and we also enjoyed the dinner in a very pretty house with a red-tiled roof. The dinner was a funny potatolike food called yucca, also rice, fried bananas, cocoanuts, chicken, and goat's milk.

As soon as dinner was over, the gang got together for the first time we'd been together without some older folks along for a long time. We took a walk down along the edge of a sugar-cane plantation, each one of us in our old clothes which our folks had made us take along so we could play a little on the farm. We were all chewing on joints of sugar cane, like we do in the United States, when pretty soon we came to a very pretty cocoanut palm tree. The next thing I knew there were only five of us on the ground. Circus had disappeared and there he was on his way up that tree. A jiffy later he was up to where the cocoanuts were, his face right beside one of them, and for a minute he looked almost like a monkey.

Say, some of those cocoanuts must have been ripe, 'cause two of them let go and came crashing down, and one of them hit me on the right foot without hurting me.

It was an interesting hike, and we planned to do it again the next day if we could. We were going to collect different kinds of flowers and leaves and press them and take them back to the United States for our folks to see and for us to talk about when we got home, like people do when they take trips and want other people to know what a good time they had. Also we were going to pick up different kinds of shells and things along the pretty little creek.

"Know what a creek is called in Spanish?" Big Jim asked all of the rest of us when we were all getting ready to go down and go in swimming that afternoon.

"What?" some of us said.

He said, "It's called a *riachuelo*."

It was a safe creek for boys to swim in, without any dangerous holes. Every boy in the world needs to have sense enough not to go in swimming in just any old place without knowing if it is safe first, and also not to go in any swimming pool without a life guard on duty. This place was as safe as our swimming hole in Sugar Creek, so we all had a grand time, making a lot of noise like we nearly always do.

That night we all slept at the mission farm under mosquito netting on very hard beds which were on very hard springs. Poetry and I had to sleep in the same hard bed.

Pretty soon when the carbide lights were out, which is the kind used out there in the country, Poetry and I crawled under the mosquito netting, let it drop down on each side of our too narrow, too hard, too noisy bed, and pulled a nice clean sheet and also a blanket up over us, and started to keep still. We were in a room all by ourselves, the rest of the gang being scattered in different missionary cabins on the school farm, although Dragonfly had a cot of his own across the room from us. Pretty soon Poetry noticed the sky which was showing through the bars of the window of our room, there not being any windowpanes in our cabin. In fact, there was hardly any window glass on nearly all of Palm Tree Island because of there not being—or not supposed to be—any flies or other flying insects —only some very small mosquitoes.

Anyway, Poetry started to quote:

> Twinkle, twinkle, little star,
>   How I wonder what you are!
> Up above the world so high,
>   Like a diamond in the sky.

When just that minute I heard someone go "Kerchew!" and it was Dragonfly on his cot across the room sneezing. Then he sneezed again and I knew he was allergic to something in that room.

I sat up and listened and strained my eyes to see if I could see him and I could there in the moonlight; also, I could hear him. He was sitting up, pushing the mosquito netting higher, 'cause it was close to his head, and I said, "What's the matter?"

He said, "I'm allergic to this mosquito netting."

Well, when a person is allergic to something and can't breathe very well, it's probably a terrible feeling. Anyway, Dragonfly said across the moonlit room to me, "I've got to get out from under this crazy net."

Right away he was out and sitting on the edge of his bed, leaning forward a little so he could breathe easier. Then he said, "Where's your flashlight, Bill?"

"What do you want it for?" I said.

"I'm going out where the air is good," Dragonfly said wheezily. It really was pitiful to see him—or *hear* him, rather, for I couldn't see him very well.

"There might be some wild animal out there," I said. "In fact, wild dogs run loose on Palm Tree Island at night." I really didn't see any sense in Dragonfly going outdoors.

"My dad gets asthma sometimes," he said, "and he always gets up, if it's summertime, and goes out into the fresh air."

Well, the air was as fresh in that room as any I'd ever breathed, but Dragonfly said he was allergic to the mosquito netting, so up we all three got and into our slippers. In the moonlight I could see us—Poetry in his striped pajamas, which made him look like a prisoner, I in mine with stripes running up and down making me look like a bean-pole, and Dragonfly with his pink ones which looked a darkish white. We went quietly to the door, opened it, and stepped out onto a tiled porch, and then down some stone steps and out under the prettiest moon you ever saw. For a minute I got to thinking about the folks back home and about Charlotte Ann lying with her face buried against her fist in her bassinet, and about my dad and mom sound asleep in their room right off our side porch. And I wondered if maybe my parents were awake wondering about me, and also worrying, especially Mom, who did most of the out-loud worrying for our family.

Anyway, there wasn't any use for me to worry about whether they were worrying about me, so I stopped worrying, but for a minute I was lonesome. We walked down toward the *rio*, sort of slow for Dragonfly's sake, although he was already better.

"Do you hear that?" Poetry said all of a sudden.

I said, "No, what?"

"Sh!" Poetry said, and I shushed, stopping stock-still and getting bumped into by Dragonfly.

We all listened a minute, and we heard a crazy sound like somebody calling for help. It was coming from a different direction than the one from which we had just come, so we knew it wasn't any of the rest of the Sugar Creek Gang calling for help and trying to fool us.

Poetry swung his flashlight around in the direction the sound was coming from and we saw, away off to the right, what looked like a strawstack at first, but which we guessed was the house of some farmer and was probably made out of the big leaves of a royal palm tree.

Pretty soon we heard the voice again, and it sounded like a ghost's voice.

"We've got to do something," Poetry said. All of a sudden his ducklike voice sounded like a man's and he said, "Come on! Follow me!"

We thought maybe we ought to go call the gang, or tell the missionary or Barry Boyland, but the noise came again and we all gasped and Dragonfly said, "My asthma's gone," which probably meant it was gone for *a while*. Somewhere I'd read or heard that when you're scared or mad or terribly excited, you can breathe easier because some of your glands called adrenal glands work faster and better when you're scared or mad or excited.

Anyway, that meant we could all run faster and get away if we had to.

So the three of us started toward that old thatched building.

Just that second a dark something came out through a place in the side of the building and darted right straight toward us and toward my flashlight which was shining right into its eyes. Then it started making a trembling-voiced noise like it was scared, or else terribly mad.

It looked like a wild animal with horns. Almost before we knew it, we were on our way down the hill, past the row of little new pine trees and were dashing back up to the cottage where we'd been staying. We were panting and scared worse than we had been for a long time. We made so much noise in spite of trying to keep quiet, that we woke up a lot of people.

Pretty soon, almost before we knew how it happened, nearly all the rest of the Sugar Creek Gang were up and standing around in their different kinds of pajamas, and a carbide light was lighted, and we were telling the whole scared story to them and to everybody that was there. But we couldn't seem to get anybody excited.

"There aren't any wild animals on this part of the island," the missionary said. "What you saw was probably one of our oxen."

"An ox can't run that fast," I said, and Dragonfly and Poetry said the same thing.

And do you know what? We couldn't get anybody to believe us, so after a while we hardly believed ourselves. Anyway, we all went back to bed, each one of us being very sleepy.

It seemed I hadn't any more than crawled under my mosquito netting and let it drop down, than I heard somebody sneezing several times in a row. I grunted and groaned, heard somebody sneeze again and again and then I knew it was Dragonfly under his mosquito netting—and it was morning.

I looked across the room at him and he was sitting up and grinning at me and Poetry, and it looked like he was feeling fine, except for having to sneeze.

Well, I heard voices outside and one of them was Little Jim's and he said, "Hey, Circus, be careful!"

Even before I knew what I was going to do, I was out from under my mosquito netting and in my bare feet walking on the cold tile floor which is what most of the good floors on the island are made of. I was across the room in a jiffy to the tall window which was not a window but a long door that reached from the floor almost to the very high ceiling. I looked out through a crack in the wooden venetian blinds which I opened and, sure enough, there was Circus halfway up a royal palm tree which grew right outside our window. And Little Jim was standing there looking up at him, and also there were several children looking up at him and jabbering something in Spanish. One of them was a girl about Circus' age, which is why all of a sudden he had probably wanted to climb the tree.

All of a sudden I wanted to be outdoors, so I made a dive for my clothes and squirmed myself into them. Then, with Poetry and Dragonfly right behind me, the three of us got out onto a tile-floored open porch and out of doors, following a stone pathway which was bordered with flowers of different kinds on either side, and were out there beside a little roadway where the children were and where the Sugar Creek Gang was. And all of us were looking at Circus who kept right on going up the royal palm tree. It was the prettiest palm tree I had ever seen in my life and the trunk of it looked like a round cement column. The top of the tree toward which Circus was climbing very fast was maybe three times higher than the missionary cabin we had stayed in that night. At the top, the big long palm leaves and their long stems looked kind of like lazy turkey feathers spread out like an umbrella in every direction.

In every direction I looked there were palm trees, looking like soldiers marching out across the fields, which were sugar-cane fields and farmlands where they grew different kinds of vegetables. Not very far away was a wooden plow that looked like some pictures I'd seen of plows that were used in Palestine where Jesus used to live while He was here on earth. There was a yoke which they said was used for oxen which pulled the plows when they plowed. On Monday we were going to see the oxen plowing and might even get a chance to drive one of them. Just that minute Dragonfly said to me, "Look, Bill! There's what we saw last night and were scared of."

"It *is* not," I said, looking at a lazy and a very

sleepy and reddish-looking ox which is a cow and which they call a *vaca* in Spanish.

Poetry pinched me and said, "Sh! I've got an idea." I shushed and kept still, and waited for a chance to be alone with Poetry when he would tell me why he had shushed me.

After a while we all had breakfast in one of the missionary homes, with every one of the Sugar Creek Gang sitting around a big wooden table in a tile-floored room. We were being waited on by some of the missionary young ladies who had come down from the United States to be missionaries. There were also two or three island girls who helped wait on the table.

And now I had better tell you what happened while we were in church about two miles from the mission station—a little church which had been made out of two houses which had once been standing side by side and fastened together. They had just knocked the wall out which had separated the two houses and that had made one big room, and it was now a church.

I never in all my whole life saw such interesting-looking boys and girls and grownup people. Every one of them had a dark face and dark hair and very pretty eyes, and every one of them sang songs like they really liked to do it better than anything in the world. I couldn't understand the words 'cause they were Spanish; but I had somebody write them down for me, and this is what they sang:

> Yo tengo vida eterna en mī corazon,
> En mi corazon, en mi corazon.
> Yo tengo vida eterna en mi corazon,
> Porque Cristo me salvo.

Which means,

> I have eternal life in my heart,
> In my heart, in my heart.
> I have eternal life in my heart,
> Because Christ saved me.

Well, Circus was going to sing a solo, and Little Jim was going to play a small folding organ for him.

The place where I was sitting was not very far from the entrance at the back of the church, and there were people all around me. All of a sudden I heard a sound of something in the road right outside the church. I forgot for a minute that Circus was singing his beautiful song which was "I will sing of my Redeemer and His wondrous love to me." I looked outside, and there, coming down the road, making a little cloud of dust, was a brown billygoat hitched up to a very small buggy which looked like a wheelchair.

8

I KNEW RIGHT AWAY it was the old man we had seen
in Palacia and whom Poetry and I had chased,
and then had gotten lost and everything. I forgot
for a minute everything that was going on in that
white-washed church—for the inside was all white-
washed—and looked at that old man. He came
driving right up close to where we were, turned into the churchyard, and turned around like he
knew exactly where he was going. Without knowing I was going to, I slipped out of my seat, and
out of doors and watched. He looked almost exactly like Old Man Paddler, and I was so sure it was
his twin brother that I didn't know what to do.

He climbed out of his buggy and was very spry
for an old man. The next thing I knew he was tying the goat to an old-fashioned hitching post which
they used to have in American towns for horses.
There were also some saddled horses there, because

a lot of the people who had come to church that day had come on horseback.

The old man turned, looked around and, with the same long machete in his hand, came hobbling up toward the church entrance. Next thing I knew I was following right along behind him. Somebody saw him coming, got up out of his seat, and let the old man have a place to sit right by the door. And I sat down just a few chairs away.

All of a sudden Circus, who was singing, "Sing, O sing, of my Redeemer," stopped and said, "Why, it's Old Man Paddler!" All the people turned around to see what he was looking at. Circus' face turned as red as a Palm Tree Island *vaca;* then he went on singing.

Even Little Jim was bothered for a minute and pressed on the wrong key.

All that time during that service and during the sermon and everything, that old man just sat there listening like he was wondering what it was all about and why he had come. He kept letting his eyes rove around at all the different things, kind of like a boy in the United States would do in church, when he didn't understand the sermon but had to keep still anyway. There really were a lot of different interesting things to look at, such as a white chicken which was just big enough to have for dinner. Without even acting scared, it came walking into the church and strolled around the aisles, his head and neck going forward and backward like chickens' heads do when they're walking. Also, there were all kinds of different colored clothes on the people, and the sermon was in Spanish, and maybe the old man couldn't hear it very well anyway, I thought.

Just outside, on the other side of the church— where I could see them through a large open door— six or seven small riding horses were tied. Also, out there was an open well with not even a pump on it. Before church had started the gang had watched the people who lived next door to the church let down a very long rope with a pail on the end of it, and draw up some very clear, clean water. They said the water was better and safer to drink if it was boiled first—some people on Palm Tree Island didn't boil their water first because of not being afraid of germs since they didn't know there were any.

While that old man wasn't listening to the sermon, and should have been because maybe he needed to, he kept looking up at the rafters of the church, which looked like the ones in our barn at Sugar Creek. Or else he would look at the people, or at the organ, or at the chicken which nobody else—except maybe a few of the Sugar Creek Gang— were looking at, and shouldn't have been. He also looked at a small black-haired baby with long black eyelashes, sleeping in its mother's arms.

Whatever made the old man not listen to the sermon? I thought, kind of disgusted at him because Dad and Mom had taught me that you are supposed to listen even when the sermon isn't very interesting.

Every now and then he would pull his machete out of its sheath, test the blade of it with his thumb to see if it was sharp, and then he would put it back in again and start to listen to the sermon again.

He didn't stay for all the church service though. Before the minister finished, the old man got up and walked out, with me following without hardly knowing I was going to do it. Then he untied his goat, climbed into his little buggy and started to drive away.

I wasn't going to let him get away this time without finding out where he lived, so I ran after him, all the time remembering a promise I'd made to Old Man Paddler in the United States, to help find his long-lost twin brother.

In a jiffy I was right beside his billy goat, just as the old man picked up the lines and clucked to the goat to start, just like Dad does to our horses at home. I said, in Spanish, *"Buenos Dias,* Senor Machete."

He looked down at me with the same kind eyes Old Man Paddler has and there was a twinkle in them as he said, *"Buenos Dias,* Bill Collins!"

"What!" I said. How'd you know my name?"

And he said, "That's easy. I read it in the *Palacia Post."* And he pulled out of his pocket a newspaper which was an English newspaper published every day in Palacia, and it gave the names of people that had come down to the island from the United States to visit, and my name was there along with all the rest of the Sugar Creek Gang.

That still didn't tell me how he knew how I was me, but maybe anybody who has ever seen red hair and freckles like mine will have a hard time to forget me.

We were maybe a hundred feet down the road where the people in the church couldn't hear us, so it was all right to talk.

The old man took hold of his reins as if he was getting ready to tell his goat to get going; then he said, "You boys stop to see me some time. I live just across the creek from the missionary. Billy and I will be pleased to see you."

Then the old man clucked to his goat, which in Spanish I had learned is called a *cabra,* and went spinning down the road back toward the place where he said he lived. Just that minute I heard somebody coming behind me, and it was Poetry, all excited and saying, "Hey! don't let him get away!" He had come as quick as he could right after he had noticed the old man and I were gone.

But I stopped Poetry from getting so excited by telling him "John Machete lives just across the creek from where we stayed last night."

Well, we kind of hated to go back into church then because of attracting so much attention and maybe interrupting the sermon. So I said, "Let's go over under that lemon tree and talk a while," which we did, there being a grapefruit tree right there also, with big, yellowish grapefruit on it, also some green ones and also some yellow ones on the ground that were already spoiling. Some people on this island didn't like grapefruit very well because of not knowing how good they were for their health.

Poetry stopped, grunted, and came back up with a big, round half-flat grapefruit in his hand. We stood there beside the tree, and were feeling fine 'cause we both thought we knew something very important. But we also were feeling just a little guilty for not being in church, the people not knowing we had to leave because of something important.

All of a sudden I heard somebody sneeze behind me and I wondered if it was Dragonfly. So I turned around, and it was.

Then I heard singing from the church and knew the sermon was over and that pretty soon church would be out and we would soon be eating dinner, which I was very hungry for right that minute. I was right, 'cause almost right away I heard the organ going and then the people were singing something which I found out was:

> Hay perdon por la sangre de Jesus
> Hay perdon por su muerte en la cruz.

and meant,

> There's pardon by the blood of Jesus,
> There's pardon by His death on the
> cross.

That is the only way anybody in the whole world, even in America, can be saved and go to heaven. Everybody in the world stays lost unless they believe that and let the Saviour pardon them.

Well, we three—Poetry, Dragonfly and I—got to the church in time to peep in and see Little Jim sitting at the organ pedaling away and a tall, blond, happy-faced missionary singing. And the people were singing too, like it was the most fun they'd had in all their lives. Also they were kind of serious faced, like they liked Somebody very much. Their faces looked like my mom's face does sometimes when she has my little baby sister Charlotte

Ann in her arms. And Charlotte Ann is asleep and mom is looking down at her and saying nothing but is happy.

The porch on which we were standing was all along the side of the church auditorium, and we were standing near the back so we could see everybody. But the people couldn't see us without turning around, which you aren't supposed to do in church anyway. Just that minute the minister had everybody shut their eyes and bow their heads. When he asked if anybody wanted to be prayed for, I saw three or four people put up their hands. One of them was a little girl sitting away down on the front row, the same girl Circus had climbed the tree for early that morning. All of a sudden Poetry said in my ear, "Look! There is some of Old Man Paddler's money being changed into Christians"; and right that minute I decided that Old Man Paddler was maybe one of the greatest men in the whole world.

A little later the meeting was over, and the people who had raised their hands went with the American missionary and a Palm Tree Island minister into a little room behind the platform to pray. For a minute I forgot about where I was, and was remembering the time when I had climbed up into our haymow back in the United States, and had gotten down on both knees in the hay and prayed. That was the time a red-haired, fiery-tempered, freckle-faced boy found out for sure that his sins were all forgiven forever.

Well, pretty soon all of us were on our way back to the mission farm for dinner. Pretty soon, also, it would be after dinner and we would go across the creek to visit the old man's house. Boy oh boy, I could hardly wait!

9

WE DIDN'T GET TO VISIT the old man that afternoon
though, 'cause just as the gang got close to his
strange-looking old house which was made out of
palm branches, he came driving around from the
corner of a barn which was made out of the same
kind of stuff the house was. The brown billy goat
was all full of pep and seemed not to even want to
stop. The old man was dressed up in white clothes
like the kind so many islanders wore.

He was polite though, and he said to us, "You
boys come back tomorrow and we'll have a visit."
He looked up at the sky and said, "This is my birth-
day, you know. Did I ever tell you I was born in
a cell of the El Torro Castle, and that I found this
lying right under me?" He showed us the machete
with the gold-inlaid handle. "Had a big gash on
my head too, right here."

The old man showed us the scar which Poetry

and I had seen in Palacia, and which started just above his right eyebrow and ran up into the place where his straw hat covered his hair.

Then without waiting for him to say, "Get up," the goat started pawing the ground and champing at the bridle bit and also started to move. And the old man let him go, waving good-bye to us with his machete.

"He's crazy," Big Jim said.

"He's mentally ill," I said.

"He has green eyes," Dragonfly said.

"He likes boys,", Little Jim said.

We watched him drive out onto the highway and start toward the suburbs of Palacia. Then we walked across the old man's yard, which didn't have any grass on it but was swept as clean as a dirt floor and had a lot of pretty flowers planted in different places.

Well, we talked about the old man a while, and we all decided that even if he did look like we thought Old Man Paddler's twin brother ought to look, he couldn't have been him 'cause his name wasn't even Paddler, and he had been born on Palm Tree Island.

"How could he be born when he was more than thirty years old?" Dragonfly asked.

"He never was a boy even," Poetry said. Then both of us—Poetry and I—told about our experience of getting lost and why. For a while the gang was pretty serious, thinking maybe the old man really was Kenneth Paddler and that he had lost his mind, and everything. We called a special gang meeting to decide what to do, all of us sitting down under a lemon tree in the old man's yard, not far from the pen where the old man kept his billy goat. We could look down the hill across the old man's yard to the creek shining in the sunlight. This time tomorrow we would all be in swimming again, then we'd come back to see the old man like he had invited us to.

Just then Dragonfly sneezed three times real fast. He looked at me kind of scared and said, "I'm allergic to billy goats," and stood up and sneezed again. That broke up our meeting, and we went home to the missionary's house.

Well, the next day came quick, and we were all getting ready to go swimming. Dragonfly was feeling fine again, but I noticed he opened his suitcase before we started and took a great big red bandana handkerchief. "I'm glad Mom made me bring it," he said to me, and for once Dragonfly's mom was right.

"Last one in's a goat's tail," I said over my shoulder to Circus, who for almost a half jiffy was running behind me, and then right away I was behind him; and then I was behind Big Jim also; and then

Poetry and I were running together, with Dragon-fly and Little Jim puffing along behind us.

Circus got to the swimming hole first; he was nearly always the fastest runner of the gang. His clothes were already almost off before he got there and in a jiffy he was out in the water splashing and saying, "The water's fine, and as warm as Sugar Creek!" I found out that it was about a minute and seventeen seconds later when I touched first one foot into the water and then the other. Then all of a sudden I was all the way in from a shove from behind which came from Poetry who had been shoved by Dragonfly.

Well, we were having fun right away, and felt right at home, in spite of the fact that we didn't know the names of any of the trees along the shore, except the palm and the seiba, and the avocado which is kind of like an elm tree, and the mahogany, out of which they make reddish furniture, and a mango tree. There were also all kinds of sweet-smelling, drooping flowers. On the other side was a banana plantation, looking a lot like an American cornfield, except that the stalks were a lot taller and the blades were about five times as wide and there were bunches of green bananas hanging from nearly every stalk.

All of us were swimming right away except Dragonfly, who I noticed was wading out carefully, holding his clothes up high above his head to keep them dry.

"What're you doing that for?" I asked.

He yelled to me and said, "We're going over to see Old John Machete, aren't we—right after a while? That means that we'll have to dress on the other side." And it did.

Dragonfly was wading on across when, all of a sudden, Circus yelled, "Hey, Gang! Look what I found!"

We all looked and saw in Circus' wet right hand something that looked like an American government bond of some kind, and I knew it was Dragonfly's lottery ticket.

Dragonfly looked at about the same time I did, and he let out a yell, "Hey!" he said. "Give me that."

"It's no good," Circus said. "I'm going to tear it up."

"It's good luck," Dragonfly said. And in a jiffy he had tossed his clothes onto the other shore and was making a dive for Circus. The two of them made a lot of noisy waves and other kinds of noise. Then Dragonfly started to sneeze and sputter and I knew he had already won his fight, 'cause Circus is a kind-hearted boy. He felt sorry for Dragonfly and let him have the worthless lottery ticket.

But it was already wet, so Dragonfly took it to

the bank and spread it out right on top of his clothes to dry. Then he came back in and we all had a lot of fun for a long time until I heard Dragonfly sneeze. I looked at him and his lips were kind of blue, which is how I knew we had all been in the water long enough.

Dragonfly was the only one who had put his clothes on the other side of the creek, so the rest of us started to wade to shore to get ours. We hadn't any more than got there when I heard Dragonfly let out a yell and a scream and start splashing to the shore on the side where his clothes were. When I looked, there, as plain as day and even plainer, was a big brown goat sniffing at his clothes; I knew right away there was going to be trouble between Dragonfly and the old man's goat.

That goat looked up at Dragonfly as if he had been interrupted in something he was thinking about; then he lowered his head again and then Dragonfly did yell. "Hey, he's chewing my lottery ticket!"

I knew that goats eat shirts and ties and old shoes and ivy and things, so I supposed he might like the taste of a lottery ticket also. And as much as I thought Dragonfly was cuckoo for wanting to save the worthless gambling ticket, I hated to see it eaten by a brown billy goat unless Dragonfly fed it to him himself.

I didn't even wait to get my clothes but started back across the little creek as fast as I could swim and wade to help Dragonfly.

That little guy was really excited, and of course that helped him from being so short of breath. And in a second, it seemed he was clambering up the bank on the other side and yelling at the goat, which wasn't a bit excited but was still chewing on the ticket.

Dragonfly must have been as mad as he had been that time back in the United States when the gang had been having a gang fight with the tough town gang. Then he had gotten socked on the side of the nose by a bully, and after that had fought like a little wildcat.

Anyway, he grabbed a stick off the ground and made a head-first dive for the goat and started hitting him on the head and horns and different places.

Well, I don't know what I would have done if I had been that goat and had been eating something I'd never tasted before and it was very good, and then something wild had come rushing at me with a club and had started to beat me in different places. I guess maybe I'd have been mad, and would have done just what that big brown, whiskered billy goat did. First, I'd have been so surprised I'd have dropped what I was eating, then I think I'd have come to my senses, if I had had any, and would have decided to fight back.

Anyway, Dragonfly had his ticket and was smoothing it out, and feeling terribly bad 'cause part of it had been chewed away, and was probably somewhere down in one of the goat's stomachs—all goats having two stomachs, one for storage and the other for digesting, just like cows do.

Right away Poetry started to quote a poem which had popped into his head, and it was:

> There was a man, whose name was Rob,
>   Who had a goat—he called him Bob.
> He loved that goat—oh yes, he did,
>   He loved that goat, just like a kid.
> One day that goat, so slick and fine,
>   Stole three red shirts from off the line.

That was as far as Poetry had gotten with his poem when I heard Circus let out a blood-curdling scream, "Hey! Dragonfly! LOOK OUT! HEY!"

Boy oh boy! That goat was mad all right. He was standing about twenty feet from Dragonfly, and was pawing the ground, and had his head down, and that meant trouble. I'd read about mad bulls and goats and how they get so mad they can't see straight, and they just lower their heads and dive right straight toward whatever they're mad at; and

102

anybody or anything that gets in the way had better not.

"RUN!" I yelled to Dragonfly.

But Dragonfly couldn't. He just stood there, looking funny, not having any clothes on. He had dropped his stick and was holding onto his lottery ticket which was already crumpled up like a girl's handkerchief after she has been crying about something, like girls do. But Circus was on the job. He really could run fast. He was out of the water right away and had a big club in his hand and was ready for the goat.

Circus could also dodge fast, and he had a good mind.

"Come on, gang!" he yelled at us. "We're going to have an old-fashioned Spanish bull fight."

Before I hardly knew what he was doing, he had run over to where Dragonfly's clothes were on the ground and had pulled out Dragonfly's great big red bandana handkerchief out of his pants' pocket. Then he was shoving Dragonfly out of the way, and waving the red handkerchief at the goat.

Well, anything red waved at a mad goat or a mad bull means the bull or the goat sees "red" and will make a head-first dive straight at whoever is waving it.

Right away the goat was mad at Circus, and his

head was down and he was running straight for him.

I saw those horns on the goat, and I knew they were dangerous, so I started screaming and screaming, "Hey, Circus, look out! LOOK OUT!"

Even before I had time to finish what I was yelling, the goat was within a few yards of Circus, who was standing stock-still, waiting. In my mind's eye I could see Circus being crashed into terribly hard and with a big hole punched in his stomach or somewhere from those goat's horns. Circus didn't even have any clothes on to protect him.

But, just like they do in a real bull fight on Palm Tree Island, Circus stepped aside, holding the handkerchief out where he had been, and the goat rushed under it like a flash of lightning and went kerswishing on past without touching Circus.

Dragonfly had already gotten out of the way. Anyway, the goat was just mad at the red handkerchief now, so he stopped about twenty feet away, looked back at Circus, saw the red handkerchief, and began to get ready to charge again—in fact, he was already ready.

Circus yelled to us then, and said, "You guys get your clothes on. Next time he charges past, I'll climb up that avocado tree, and we'll be all right."

Well, that was a good idea, 'cause I knew Circus could climb fast.

I guess maybe it would have worked all right, but Circus slipped and fell just as the goat was getting ready to make another charge at him. And that's where I got myself into trouble—because of being impulsive, and also because of liking Circus so well. I didn't want anything to happen to him, and also I was closer to Circus than any of the rest of the gang.

I just couldn't stand to see anything happen to him, so I dived in, grabbed the handkerchief myself, and—well, that was how the goat happened to be mad at me instead of at Circus and Dragonfly.

I got scared and started to run. I also remembered that I had red hair as well as Dragonfly's red handkerchief.

I turned and started toward the old man's house.

"Run faster!" Dragonfly yelled to me.

"Stop!" Circus yelled. "Wave your flag and dodge."

But my tangled-up brain told me to keep on running which I did.

I guess Old John Machete must have heard something going on, or else he wanted to get his goat to hitch it up and take a ride, 'cause right that minute he came out of his thatched house and started out across his pretty yard which didn't have any grass, but had been swept as clean as I knew the dirt floor of his house was.

10

WITH DRAGONFLY YELLING for me to run and Circus yelling even louder for me to stop and wave the red flag, I didn't know what to do. So I kept on doing what I was doing, which was running. It seemed like if I would run right straight toward the old man I wouldn't be in as much danger as if I ran in some other direction, so I kept on going.

Also, nearly all the gang was yelling at me to do different things, so I didn't do any of them but kept right straight on toward the old man. Also, I was yelling myself—anyway, trying to—only it was like being in a dream when some fierce wild animal is after me and I can't run very fast, and I get more and more scared until I wake up. Only now I had sense enough to know that I wasn't dreaming and that I was as awake as I ever was. I thought if the goat really socked me like they do in comic-strip pictures which people draw, I'd probably get hurt terribly bad.

"*Help!*" I yelled to the old man. But he just stood there, kind of shading his eyes, standing not very far from a very pretty rose bush, which was close to a wooden plow and a wooden ox yoke.

I don't know what made me do it—I certainly didn't have any sense to do what I did, and it certainly wasn't fair for me to do it. I should have run for a tree and swung myself around behind it and let the goat ram himself head first into the tree, but I didn't. Instead I ran straight for Old John Machete, maybe because I knew he knew the goat and the goat might stop and start to behave himself.

A jiffy later I reached the old man, made a swoop around him like he was a tree trunk, and stopped right behind him.

Well, the goat was running terribly fast, and was so mad he was blind I guess. Anyway, the next thing I knew he had run kersquash right into old John Machete, who was already halfway turned around before I dived for him. Then he had swung around the other half, and right then the goat struck him. Just like the old man was a straw dummy or a scarecrow in a garden, he toppled over. His hands flew around up in the air, and he fell kersquash-wham thud-thud over the old plow. He kind of turned a little while he was falling and down he went face first. Even before he got all the way down, I knew it was going to happen. I just *knew* it. He was going to get terribly hurt.

I was already screaming because of being scared myself. Then all of a sudden I started screaming again, 'cause there the old man was, all sprawled out half on and half off the plow and his head struck against one end of it.

I guess they call it being hysterical when a boy feels like I did. Because when I saw that old man fall so hard on his head and I thought how terribly bad he might be hurt and what if he was Old Man Paddler's brother and might even die, I started to cry and laugh, first one and then the other, and felt weak in the knees, and for a minute I didn't know where I was. I felt like I was going to faint or something. Then, like my mind had made a dive into a dark tunnel, I didn't know anything—in fact, I didn't even know I didn't know anything.

The next thing I did know, I was lying flat on the ground and somebody was pouring water on my face and neck, and somebody whose voice sounded like it was Big Jim's, was saying, "He's coming to; he's opening his eyes," which I was and which I did right that minute. Right away I was sitting up and looking around and feeling dizzy in the head.

"Where—what happened?" I started to ask, then stopped 'cause right then I saw the scared look on the rest of the gang's faces. I also saw the brown billy goat not very far away chewing on some leaves that hung low from a lemon tree. Then I remembered the old man and swung around just in time to hear him groan and groan again like he had been terribly hurt. Then he started talking and saying, "You've got to let me out of this cell, gentlemen. I tell you I am not a spy, but am a citizen of the United States. I'm a newspaperman."

Then he lay back again, gasping for breath, not saying anything for a minute. Then right away he started in again, saying, "Let me out of here! I'm not who you think I am! I tell you. I'm—oh, my head! My head!"

He started to half talk and half cry again and said, "I tell you, those pictures are for an American newspaper."

All of a sudden the old man twisted himself to a sitting position, and raised one brown hand up to his forehead where he had been hurt. He stared for a minute at us, and then he groaned again and turned pale around the eyes and just wilted back against Big Jim's shoulder like a tree falling along Sugar Creek.

"He's fainted again," Poetry said beside me, and he had.

Well, we had to do something. I still didn't feel very good because of having just fainted myself, but

I knew what a guy ought to do when a guy has just fainted. So I said, "Let's get his head lower than the rest of his body," which we started to do. But the old man hadn't fainted!

Right that minute he opened his eyes and stared around at us and at things just as if he'd never seen us or his garden or house before.

He looked scared for a minute, also he looked so fierce that I got the queerest feeling inside like I was looking at a wild man instead of at old John Machete.

"We've got to get him out of the sun," Big Jim said. And he was right 'cause the sun was shining right straight down on him and into his face. But we didn't even have time to carry him over under the lemon tree to the shade or to try to get him into his house. For right that minute he opened his eyes and swung his arms out like he was fighting to get away from a lot of people. And almost before we could get out of the way of his flying fists to keep from getting hurt, he twisted around, scrambled to his feet which had new, American-looking shoes on them, and started across the yard toward his old thatched-roofed house, calling out like a wild man.

He wasn't going straight though, but was staggering this way and that like Circus' dad used to stagger when he came out of a beer parlor before he became a Christian and God had cleaned him up inside so he didn't drink anymore.

He stopped right in front of the old wooden door and stared at it like he had never seen it before. Then he staggered forward again, and the next thing I knew he was inside. The door went shut after him with a bang, with all of us on the outside.

Well, there we were, all of us, staring at each other and wondering what had happened and what we ought to do and how quick we ought to do it.

"Let's go get Mr. Fisher," Dragonfly said. Mr. Fisher was the missionary's name. Then Dragonfly sneezed three times real quick. His teeth were chattering, he was so scared.

"Think we're a bunch of sissies?" Circus said in a half-mad voice. And the way he said it made everyone of us decide that not a one of us was.

"He sure is crazy," Poetry said, and looked at me.

I said, "He's mentally ill."

Little Jim piped up and said with tears in his voice, "What—what'll Old Man Paddler say if he finds out his brother is crazy?"

I'd forgotten for a minute that that was who I thought the old man was, so that started us all to talking and Big Jim called a meeting.

We couldn't take time to use all the rules of what is called an official meeting. Big Jim said to us, "Didn't we plan to all come over and see the old man right after we'd been in swimming?"

We all said, "Yes."

Big Jim said, "Well, then, what are we waiting for? Why don't we go in and see him? Anybody here afraid to?"

I looked at Little Jim and he was looking all around him for something, and I knew he was looking for a stick to carry; but there wasn't any. I felt sorry for him 'cause always around Sugar Creek he carried a stick; that's one reason why he was so brave whenever he was in any danger.

Just that minute Big Jim looked at all of us and said in a thundery voice, "Are we afraid or aren't we? Are we going in to see the old man or not?"

I felt something hot running up and down my trembling spine and I spoke up real quick, "We're going in!"

My voice was almost drowned out by the rest of the gang's voices which had said the same thing as loud as I had: *"We're going in!"*

11

WELL, I WAS VERY BRAVE while Big Jim's voice made me feel that way, but I hadn't any sooner said, "We're going in," than I was scared, 'cause I'd never been inside a palm-leaf house where a crazy man lived. So when we all started to walk along behind each other to that old wooden door, I began to feel my heart pounding and pounding. And I was also feeling my fists all doubled up as if I was going to be in a fight or something.

About twenty feet from the door, Big Jim stopped us and looked around to see if we were all there and all brave enough to go in; all of us acted like we were. Just like they had done once before in the United States, he and Circus went up to the door first and knocked, and called, "May we come in?"

Nobody must have answered 'cause Big Jim turned the old-fashioned doorknob and pushed open the door, stepping back at the same time, and

I got a look inside. All I could see though was a dirt floor that was swept as clean as the yard we were standing in, and there was a long room with several old wooden stiff-backed chairs beside a table.

"Hello!" Big Jim called, *"Buenas tardes!"*

But there wasn't any answer.

So Big Jim called again, and when nobody answered, he pushed the door open still further. And then we all heard it at the same time, I guess. The sound was coming from another room somewhere in the house, and it sounded like *"Help!"*

Well, we knew we had to do something. So in we all went, following Big Jim, who picked up one of the old wooden chairs which I noticed had a calf-skin leather seat, just in case he had to use it to protect himself.

It was the craziest looking house I ever saw, a little bit like one of the straw sheds we have on our farm at Sugar Creek when my dad builds a little shed out of boards, leaving big cracks between, and then has straw blown all over it with the blower of a threshing machine. When you're on the inside, all you can see are the boards or poles, and also the cracks between, which are all covered over with straw—only John Machete's house had palm leaves *instead* of straw all over the boards and poles.

Big Jim whirled around and held up his finger to all of us to keep still while he and Circus crept toward the other room.

Even while I was scared and my teeth were chattering, I noticed that that other room toward which Big Jim and Circus were creeping was really just another thatched house right beside the one we were in. The eve of its roof had come down to meet the eve of the roof of the house we were in, and right between the two hung a big split royal palm log. All royal palm trees were hollow on the inside, somebody had told us, kind of like a cane fishing pole, only they don't have any joints like fishing poles have.

Right that minute Poetry, who didn't act scared at all, whispered in my ear and told me what the log was for. He said, "That's called a 'canal,' 'cause it's hung there to catch the water which runs down the roofs of the two houses, and it falls in the hollow log and runs away instead of inside." That sounded like good sense.

I started to think about how smart the island people were, when the old man interrupted my thoughts by saying to Big Jim and Circus, who had just stepped inside, "Who are you? What do you want? Where am I? How did I get here?"

My eyes saw the long-whiskered old man sitting in a corner of his room beside a long table which had a little hole in the center of its top, and a little fire of live coals was in the hole. I knew it was a charcoal fire like they had in the missionary home; most islanders use charcoal stoves to cook with.

In the old man's hands was his machete with its gold-inlaid-handle. And he looked at us like he would use it on the first one of us who got too close to him or who might do anything he didn't like.

Well, he had asked four questions—"Who are you? What do you want? Where am I? How did I get here?" So we just stared at him and he at us, and he held onto his machete.

Just then Little Jim piped up and said, "We're the Sugar Creek Gang from the United States, and we're Christians and won't hurt you."

You should have seen the strange look that came into the old man's eyes when Little Jim said that. We all almost jumped out of our skins and we couldn't believe our ears when he said, "The last time I was in Sugar Creek was two years ago just before I came down here."

The very second the old man said "Sugar Creek," he got a scared look in his eyes again and his old hands gripped his machete, like he was expecting to have to use it any minute.

He wasn't looking at us though, but was looking between my and Big Jim's heads at something or somebody behind us. The look in his eyes was like he was seeing a ghost or maybe a dead man.

Right away I thought, *Is somebody coming into the room, or is some fierce person standing behind me—maybe ready to do something to all of us?* Being in a foreign country made it easy for me to be scared, when I was already scared anyway. The look in his eyes was so fierce for a minute that I was afraid to turn around. I felt my knees getting weak like I was going to slide down kerplop on the swept dirt floor.

All of us must have thought the old man was looking at something behind us 'cause Dragonfly turned around quick to see what was there, and the rest of us did the same thing. But shucks! It wasn't anything at all. Nobody was coming into the room, and all that we could see was a mirror on the wall— just an ordinary looking glass, maybe about the size of the one that hangs on our bathroom wall in our house at home.

"Who—who is that?" the old man cried, and staggered out of his chair and started toward the mirror.

Well, everything was still crazy and so also was the old man, I thought. He had his machete in his hands and he wasn't paying any attention to any of us, only looking with a crazy expression in his eyes at the mirror.

Then I heard him let out a terrible cry like he was seeing a real ghost, and what he said was, "It's *me!* I'm an old man! *I'm an old man!*" He almost screamed the words.

Then he staggered back away from the mirror like he was afraid of it. He raised his hand up to his forehead to the place where he had been struck when he had fallen over the plow; and then, just like everything in the room was going around and around in his mind, he swayed a little and, like a tired old maple tree along Sugar Creek, he started to fall again. Before any one of us could get to him, he had crumpled to the floor.

"Quick!" Big Jim ordered. *"You,* Bill! Run and get Mr. Fisher. We've got to get him into the mission hospital."

Imagine me running! I certainly didn't feel like it. I didn't feel like anything, but something had to be done. So I whirled around, dived under the canal and into the other room, dodged the table there and the other wooden chair which also had a calf-skin seat, and swished through the still open door, out across the old man's yard, dodging rose bushes and flowers of different kinds, running lickety-sizzle toward the creek. I knew where there was a place where I could get across on some stones at a narrow, shallow place, which the gang had found on Saturday. I had to pass the swimming hole first though, and right there is where I stumbled over something and fell down, tumbling over myself and hurting my knees. I scrambled to my feet and looked around to see what I had stumbled over and it was a—I could hardly believe my eyes. It was an honest to goodness cane fishing pole like the kind we used at Sugar Creek. Somebody had been fishing with it, in fact had set and left it. There was a line on it, and the very minute I scrambled to my feet that pole started to wiggle and act funny like it was alive, and then I looked out into the water and sure enough there was a fish out there in the water somewhere on the line. Even while I was scared and worried and hurrying to get the missionary, I was all of a sudden lonesome for home again and wanted to get back to Sugar Creek and go fishing.

As much as I wanted to stay stopped and catch that fish, I didn't dare. I came right away to the place where there were stones across the narrow place and whisked across and ran like a deer for the hospital.

I came panting up past a windmill which was used to pump water for the mission, and rushed up to the pretty red-tile-roofed missionary cabin, calling: "Mr. Fisher! Mr. Fisher! Come *quick!* John Machete has gone crazy, and has fainted and is dangerous and might kill somebody!"

12

WELL, WE GOT THE OLD MAN to the hospital, and it looked as if he was a lot worse than just being mentally ill. They kept him there all the rest of that day, and also the next and the next; and all he did was wake up and go to sleep and wake up and go back to sleep, and talk about Sugar Creek. Once when I was standing in the doorway looking in at him as he lay there asleep in his clean white cot, he woke up and said to the missionary nurse, "Bring me the morning paper."

The missionary nurse had one lying on a table close by and it was a copy of the Palacia paper I'd seen before. Old John Machete looked at it and said, "That's all wrong! The date is wrong!"

Then he let the paper fall onto his cot, and it slid off and onto the floor, and he went back to sleep again.

Just that minute Mr. Fisher came in and he and

the nurse started talking quietly not far from where I was and I heard them say to each other, "Looks like amnesia. He may be an American."

Well, when I heard that, I was so excited I could hardly sit still for wanting to dive out of doors and hurry to the gang and tell them what I'd heard and that maybe we'd actually found Old Man Paddler's twin brother.

Right away I was outside and running lickety-sizzle along a little path that ran from the hospital to the missionary's cabin to where I knew the gang was supposed to be taking their siestas. I was supposed to be taking mine too, but I wasn't because I'd been down talking to the kind of pretty nurse, because of her having red hair like mine and also because of my wanting to find out what they had found out about the old man, but mostly because of not wanting to take a siesta.

But I had something to tell the gang now, I thought, as my feet flew up the path to where the gang was. In a jiffy I was across the tile-floored open porch and through the door into the big airy tile-floored room where the gang would be trying to sleep. The very minute I came bursting in, I half yelled to the gang, "Old John Machete is Old Man Paddler's twin brother!"

Dragonfly was the only one of the gang who wasn't asleep. He was sitting up on the edge of his cot under the open window and was blowing his nose with a big red handkerchief.

The gang woke up, each one in a different way. Poetry grunted, groaned and rolled over with a jerk which shook his cot; then he shoved a fist into his pillow and started to sleep again. Little Jim, who was sleeping on his back, just opened his eyes, blinked them at me, blinked twice more and started to rub his eyes awake.

Circus was wide awake quick, and rolling over and out of bed in a hurry. He was feeling so fine he looked up at the rafters which were stretched across the room above his head like he wished he was up there. That is, he looked like it for only a minute until he saw what I saw at the same time. It was a great big spider almost as big as Little Jim's hand when it is spread out—or, anyways, as big as my little baby sister Charlotte Ann's hand.

"Look!" Circus cried. "A spider!" Maybe Circus remembered the black widow spider which had bitten his dad once in the United States and almost killed him.

Right away we were all awake and all of us looking at the terribly big spider.

Just then Dragonfly sneezed twice and looked up at the rafter and at the spider and said, "I'll bet I'm allergic to—"

Well, we'd heard him say he was allergic so

much that we all were tired of it, so he didn't get to finish his sentence because of one of the gang's pillows going kerplop into his face before he could.

"Honest," I said, "They've just found out Old John Machete is Old Man Paddler's brother and—"

And right away that was the end of their siestas. You should have heard us talking and talking and still talking and deciding—even before the doctor and the nurse did—that we were right.

Anyway, this story is getting too long, but that's actually what they found out—that Old Man Paddler's brother had come down to Palm Tree Island to get an important news story, and he had been arrested for being a spy and had been put in a cell in El Torro Castle. He had tried to get out and had been hit on the head with a blunt instrument of some kind. The shock had been so much for him that it was like shutting a little door in one room of his brain, and he couldn't remember who he was, or where he came from. In fact, he had been a little goofy for all the years between then and now.

"He came out here and built a house along the creek and did a lot of fishing, because when a man has amnesia he likes to do what he *used* to like to do," Poetry said, having read a story in a magazine about amnesia one time.

"Won't Old Man Paddler be tickled?" Little Jim

said. "I'll bet they'll go fishing together again like they used to when they were just our size and used to live and play together along Sugar Creek."

All of a sudden Poetry said, "I'm homesick. I want to go home and go swimming in Sugar Creek."

"It'll be wintertime when we get home," I said. *"I'm* lonesome for a *snowdrift."*

Dragonfly sneezed twice, and it's a good thing there wasn't any snowdrift right there then, or maybe he would have fallen head first into the middle of it—and I know which one of the Sugar Creek Gang would have made him do it.

We were all on the old man's side of the river now, not very far from the place where we had had the interesting experience with the goat. The old man's goat was in its pen now, and the wind was blowing our way, which is maybe why Dragonfly was sneezing worse than usual. But he was feeling good anyway—in fact, all of us were.

Just that minute we heard the goat baa a few times and Dragonfly, all of a sudden, took out his red handkerchief, and said, "I told you my lottery ticket meant good luck!"

"It did not," I said. "It almost got us all killed!"

Dragonfly set his face, and then he got a mischievous twinkle in both his Dragonflylike eyes and said, "Yes, but if I hadn't kept it, and if the goat hadn't tried to eat it, and if the old man hadn't gotten knocked over and bumped his head, he wouldn't have had the amnesia knocked out of him."

I just stared at him, disgusted, but he wasn't through talking. He said, "It's also a good thing I found that lucky horseshoe at home before I came, 'cause that helped Mom to decide to let me come. And if I hadn't come, there wouldn't have been any lottery ticket for the goat to eat and there wouldn't have been any red handkerchief and there wouldn't have been any—"

That was as far as Dragonfly got, for Poetry was reminded of the old woman who went to market, and he started to say,

> The rat began to gnaw the rope, the rope began to hang the butcher, the butcher began to kill the cow, the cow began to drink the water, the water began to put out the fire, the fire began to burn the stick, the stick began to beat the dog, the dog began to bite the pig, the pig began to jump over the style, and they all got home that night.

"Let's all go in swimming," Circus said, and already he was on his way to the creek.

It would be our last swim before going back to America. Boy oh boy, I was glad we were going home! We'd all had a swell time on Palm Tree Island, learning and doing a lot of things, and seeing what it is like to be in a foreign country. Maybe I'd be a foreign missionary myself, some day, I thought, and Little Jim had already made up his mind he was going to be one.

Right after we finished swimming we all had supper, which was corn and rice and fried bananas and cocoanuts and also a very good cold drink called *limonada bien fria,* which means good cold lemonade.

"I'd rather have sassafras tea up in Old Man Paddler's cabin," Little Jim said and nudged me. I looked down at his face, and he had a homesick expression in his eyes.

Along with the lemonade we had *torta con helado,* which was cake and ice cream and, boy oh boy, was it good. The missionary family actually had a refrigerator which runs with kerosene which some kind Christian in the United States had paid for, and I knew who it was.

Even eating the ice cream made me homesick, and I was glad we were going to get to go home soon. But if I had known what was going to happen about a week after we got home and started going to school again, I wouldn't have been so happy.

But of course I didn't know either that our very

pretty schoolteacher, whom we all liked better than any we'd ever had, was going to get married at Christmastime and that a man teacher was going to take her place. Imagine that! A *man* teacher for a country school! For the school the Sugar Creek Gang all had to go to!

But that's getting into my next story almost before it happened, so I'll have to stop right now and wait till later when I get more time, which I hope will be almost right away because of it being so important.

Moody Press, a ministry of the Moody Bible Institute, is designed for education, evangelization and edification. If we may assist you in knowing more about Christ and the Christian life, please write us without obligation to: Moody Press, c/o MLM, Chicago, Illinois 60610.